LOVE IS ENOUGH

LOVE IS ENOUGH

Denise Robins

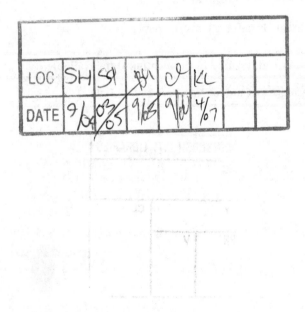

LOC	SH	SI			KL		
DATE	9/02	03/05	9/05	9/06	4/07		

CHIVERS
THORNDIKE

This Large Print edition is published by BBC Audiobooks Ltd, Bath, England and by Thorndike Press, Waterville, Maine, USA.

Published in 2004 in the U.K. by arrangement with the Author's Estate.

Published in 2004 in the U.S. by arrangement with Claire Lorrimer.

U.K. Hardcover ISBN 0–7540–9908–3 (Chivers Large Print)
U.K. Softcover ISBN 0–7540–9909–1 (Camden Large Print)
U.S. Softcover ISBN 0–7862–6282–6 (General)

The text of this Large Print edition is unabridged.
Other aspects of the book may vary from the original edition.

Set in 16 pt. New Times Roman.

Printed in Great Britain on acid-free paper.

British Library Cataloguing in Publication Data available

Library of Congress Control Number: 2003115692

CHAPTER ONE

'Miss Lorraine, Mr. Walton wants you.'

Fleur Lorraine looked up from the long strip of film on which she had been working steadily since nine o'clock that morning and nodded in reply to the summons to her chief's office. It was now late in the afternoon and she felt really tired. She had hoped to go home early, but if Mr. Walton, head of the film-developing department, wanted her it was pretty sure to mean more work.

That meant no use complaining about a possible trip home in an overcrowded bus in the blackout. The family had learned to expect her return at any time of the day or night and they would not worry. Quite cheerfully she laid down the celluloid strip and made her way through the rambling building to Mr. Walton's office. The rooms were in their usual state of bustle and excitement. On her left she passed the studio where the new producer had just been directing a scene in the latest picture which the company was making. The set was a desert scene. Sand dunes, palms, blue skies. A really brilliant example of the scene-builder's craft. Most of that afternoon Fleur had heard the studio orchestra playing sad Eastern music which was supposed to increase the emotional output of the leading lady who was known to be more of a social beauty than an actress.

Fleur shared the contempt of the secretarial and camera executives who openly sneered at the new mushroom-star who had to be coaxed out of her habitual lethargy. The woman had a golden opportunity. Money, clothes and influence were on her side. If only she could be persuaded to use her brains, to be natural and human, she would bring fame to herself and business to the studios.

It had always been Fleur's ambition to act for the screen. An ambition, she was realist enough to know, that was not likely to be gratified. For the last ten months she had been working at the Filmograph Studios in Balham, first of all doing office work and more recently joining up pieces of developed film. It was a difficult, trying job and not particularly well paid. And nobody seemed to have noticed that she was extraordinarily pretty, nor had anyone troubled to find out whether or not she might have some dramatic talent. Nobody worried about her.

Fleur was left to worry about herself; which she did frequently. She was determined not to remain in her present position for one moment longer than was necessary, and Fleur, besides being very pretty, was a far-sighted girl with plenty of intelligence and personal charm.

She loved to act behind the closed door of her bedroom in her father's house at Streatham Hill, to put on one of her few evening frocks and, winding a chiffon scarf around her head, walk up and down in front of her mirror with tragic expressions, pretending that she was a thousand-pounds-a-week star rehearsing her latest heart-drama. For Fleur, these moments in the seclusion of her room were really thrilling. She was, in fact, an actress born. Yet she worked under the very eyes of Filmograph's most highly paid talent-scouts without the fact that she was better than the leading-lady being realised.

At home, where she lived with her invalid mother and eighteen-year-old sister, Fleur was the one to manage the little villa, to plan the meals and, more often than not, cook them on her return from the studios.

This afternoon she felt suddenly elated when she paused outside Mr. Walton's office. She could hear men's voices and knew that a group of them would be in there, talking and smoking. The 'Big Three' had been in conference most afternoons that week. It would be a splendid opportunity to meet her chiefs and try to get them to display some slight spark of interest in her. She must try to make an impressive entrance, she told herself.

Having knocked on the frosted door marked 'Private', she shut it firmly behind her and walked across the heavily carpeted room.

'You sent for me,' she said in her soft, well-modulated voice, and stood with her head flung back as though posing for one of the

3

cameras in the studio.

The three men who looked towards her were of varied types but each in his own way bore the indefinable stamp of the film world. Mr. Walton, thin, sleek-haired, and perfectly groomed, sat with cigar in his mouth at his desk, drumming on a blotter with a gold pencil; Mark Manton, the company's ace publicity-man, stood lounging against the back of a chair which housed the long, untidily clothed limbs of Raymond Summers, who was the accepted authority on all matters relating to scenery and design. He was the antithesis of Mr. Walton. Blue polo jersey, old grey slacks, rough, curly hair. Pipe between his teeth.

There was silence in the smoke-filled office as all eyes were directed towards the girl who, up till this moment, nobody had noticed and who had been just one of the countless workers in the studios who had to be paid every Friday night. The warm spring sunshine streamed through the window and fell upon her, throwing up the vivid tints in chestnut hair which waved crisply over tiny ears. Her skin was camellia white, her cheeks warmed with a colour which could only be her own. Her eyes, large and dark, were deep-set and thick-lashed, under narrow crescent brows; her mouth, a red, inviting curve, half open to reveal small, even teeth. Even these men, used to perfection, saw real loveliness in Fleur's slender waist, straight shoulders, perfect legs.

4

Here was really beauty indeed, and all three in the office recognised the fact. Fleur stood for a moment, almost conscious of the impression she had made. Then Mr. Walton broke the tension by coughing and turning his eyes from her, Raymond Summers made a mental painting of her for future use, and Mark Manton looked from the flushed, eager young face and was instinctively relieved to find small, rounded ankles and narrow little feet.

'The girl's a beauty,' he mumbled to himself. 'A peach.'

'Miss Lorraine,' Walton said, 'I want that last roll of film you were working on. Did they tell you to bring it?'

'No,' said Fleur; 'but I'll get it at once.'

She turned and walked out, and as she closed the door behind her, heard Raymond Summers' voice:

'You fellows beat me,' he was saying. 'You spend weeks searching the country for the right lead in the film. Then you sign up the Langton woman at two hundred a week, when all the time you had the ideal girl under your very noses.'

Fleur paused, her heart racing violently with excitement. She *must* wait to hear Manton's reply, she thought. She *must*. Manton probably had more influence than any other man in the film world. His answer came in that curiously slow, deep voice which held more than a touch

5

of American drawl.

'Summers is right. Why the hell haven't we noticed that kid before? What's her name, Walton?'

'Fleur Lorraine,' said Walton.

'French, or is it really Nelly Jones?'

'No. It's her real name. Her father is French. I remember I had her in here to take a call from Paris. She can speak the lingo, too. Her own father died in Paris and she made all the arrangements—first-class business woman—that baby! And her French is as good as her English, and that's saying something.'

Moving across the room, Mark Manton smote the desk with his fist.

'Saying something,' he repeated violently. *I'll* say it's saying something. Here we have June Langton playing the part of a woman who is supposed to be able to speak three languages. Three languages, my foot! I'm no scholar, but it brings tears to my eyes to hear her trying to mouth *"Je vous aime"* in the first shot.'

Walton held up a hand as though to restrain the flow of words from the publicity man's lips.

'I see your point, Mark. This Lorraine girl might have been O.K. But it's a bit late to think about what we might have done. We happen to be under contract to pay June Langton two hundred a week until the film is made. That's a lot of money.'

'It's a hell of a lot of money,' Manton

6

returned. 'You don't need to tell me. But let *me* tell *you* it's a drop in the bucket compared with what we stand to lose if this picture flops. And, if you ask me, this Langton dame is already half-way to killing it stone dead.'

'I agree there,' Summers said quickly. 'No good spoiling the ship for two hundred a week.'

Walton moved uncomfortably in his chair and fumbled in his case for a cigarette.

'I'd hate to break the news to La Langton,' he said, with a thin smile.

Manton gave a harsh laugh.

'Leave that bit of it to me, George. I owe that young woman a few cracks. The poor dear couldn't walk on in a Mayfair Repertory company and know to what to do with her hands. But this girl . . . perfect! Face, figure, voice. Perfect, I tell you!'

Fleur did not wait to hear any more, but fled with burning cheeks and tingling pulses to the peace of her own office. A panic of excitement possessed her. With any luck, and not too much opposition from Walton, she might be on the road to success.

Just how far she had travelled along the road she was not to know until the following morning. She had hardly slept all night, instinctively feeling that her lucky star was in the ascendant. At ten o'clock the next day, a warm, brilliant day, when Londoners sweltered in the heat and thought wistfully of cool blue seas and meadows starred with daisies, Fleur was sent for and asked to present herself in Mark Manton's office.

Face to face with Manton, Fleur felt herself become suddenly cold with nerves and sat staring at the publicity-man with her dark, ardent eyes. He smiled at her encouragingly.

'Don't look so scared, Miss Lorraine. What I'm going to say to you will probably be a shock—but I imagine a pleasant one. I'm going to tell you right away that you are the girl we want to play lead in our present production.'

'Oh!' she said weakly, and felt her heart hammering.

'You can act, can't you?' he asked.

'I—I think so,' she stammered.

'I think so too,' said Manton. 'You came into Walton's room last night like a tragedy queen. Fine, it was. And you've got the right colouring. Deep-set eyes, high cheek-bones, a perfect set of teeth. You should be photogenic. Anyhow, I shall have some tests taken of you this morning. Whether you have experience or not doesn't matter. The part we are going to offer you is a natural one.'

'Tell me about it,' said Fleur breathlessly.

Manton leaned back in his revolving chair and clipped the end from a cigar. He told her about the part, and to Fleur it sounded more like a dream than a real offer. The directors had agreed to put her in that part. They were willing to pay off June Langton and to scrap the part of the film in which she had appeared. But the producer had reminded them that Fleur Lorraine was a name which meant exactly nothing to the public, and that it was Manton's job to see that it should be made into a household word by the time the film was ready to be launched.

Last night Manton had evolved a big publicity stunt which they intended to put into action. His idea was that Fleur should be packed off to the smartest hotel in Monte Carlo, where she would pose as Princess Olga—or some such name—a princess of a fictitious lost European State. When she had been living there long enough to become notorious (she would have all the clothes and jewels she needed) she would suddenly disappear. Rumour would be worked up to the effect that the princess had been captured or kidnapped. At the height of the sensation the film which would solve the mystery would have its world première. The directors fully expected that such a result would be a sensational box-office draw.

'The whole of Europe and Hollywood will ring with it,' Manton finished enthusiastically. 'Photographs, columns about the missing princess, will fill the papers. It will be front page news. Think, my dear, of the sensation which will be caused when the film is released!'

9

Fleur listened in rapt attention, her cheeks aglow with excitement and anticipation.

'It sounds too marvellous!' she exclaimed. 'I can't begin to tell you what I feel about it all. My only fear is that I may be unable to make the grade.'

'Nonsense,' Manton replied, with a shake of his head 'That need be the least of your worries. You will merely go to Monte Carlo and act your part. I, myself, intend to go with you as your private secretary, and so direct your movements without raising any suspicion that it is a stunt.'

Fleur swallowed hard. A picture of the sun-drenched harbour at Monaco swam before her eyes. She had read that there was no blackout on the Italian frontier, no repercussion of war. There would be only gaiety and sunshine and the ever-present knowledge that her foot was firmly planted on the first rung of the ladder which led to fame.

'You are certainly very encouraging,' she smiled.

'Then you will do it?' Manton said, leaning towards her. 'We'll pay you a nominal sum while you're abroad. When you begin working on your part we will talk about real money. It's your chance, my dear, the chance of a lifetime.'

'I realise that. I can only say that I accept your offer—and thank you.'

For a moment Mark Manton looked at her

in silence, and something more than a keen eye to business moved him. He did not only see Fleur Lorraine as a possible box-office draw, but as a woman to be sought after and won. Her slim, lovely figure, her warm chestnut hair, those great brown eyes under their long lashes—why, he asked himself once again, had he not noticed her before? She was exquisite. There was a certain air of eager youth, of enchanting innocence about her which could not fail to appeal to him.

Fleur had noticed the almost imperceptible change of expression which had crossed Mark's face as he looked at her—and was not surprised. It was public knowledge that the middle-aged publicity-man was a bachelor with a list of rather tawdry affairs on the red side of his balance. Manton was a hard man. Hard to look at with his narrow eyes, thin, sensuous lips and smooth black hair which was already beginning to grey at the temples. Some women raved about him and admitted that they found him attractive and good-looking. Fleur found him neither. He was a type that could never appeal to her. Too self-satisfied, too blatantly worldly and calculating. But this morning his personal life did not worry her. She felt quite capable of handling any man, and she was not regarding him as a man—only as an important factor in this big new chance of her existence.

She was neither astonished nor afraid when he suddenly put down his cigar and, leaning

11

forward, laid a hand over one of hers.

'I know we'll get along well,' he said. 'The company will pay all expenses. You will live like a princess and I in your suite as your secretary. It should be lots of fun, baby.'

Fleur drew away her hand.

'I'm sure it will.'

'Yes, the new Fleur Lorraine and I will have a grand time. By the way, I like the name Fleur. Why not keep it? Princess Fleur sounds pretty good.'

She laughed and shrugged her shoulders.

'Why not? The whole thing sounds so unreal that I can hardly credit it. Can you tell me when it begins?'

'Right now,' he answered unexpectedly. 'Tomorrow you can start looking for clothes and whatever else you may require. You can spend what you like. I'll ask Germaine, who is dressing the film, to give you a hand. You will have a few weeks to yourself while I fix up exit and money permits.'

Fleur stood up, almost dazed by the realisation of the turn which events had taken, and Manton, looking at her once again, thought how much he was going to enjoy life on the Côte d'Azur with this new-found protégée. His only regret was the thought of the weeks which must elapse until they could leave. He could, of course, take her around London, but that, he knew, would not be intelligent of him. Not until they were in

Monte Carlo would he reveal his feelings. Then the magic of the south, the stars and the Mediterranean would be his allies. He visualised dinner at the *Château de Madrid*, where they would look down from the stone terrace which seemed to be suspended over a sheet of jewelled velvet; the drive back along the winding Corniche road; liqueurs at that strange little Monégasque café on the Condamine; a touch of Mediterranean madness—and Fleur Lorraine would be in his arms.

Aloud he said casually:

'Are you engaged to be married, by any chance?'

'No,' she said, shaking her head, 'I am not.'

'How's that? Are all the men around here blind?'

Fleur laughed.

'Not blind—only careful!'

Manton picked up his cigar and gave the ash a minute examination. His hard, blunt face took on a wary expression.

'Well, now I must get down to some work,' he said curtly. 'You'd better go and clear things up in your office—then get hold of Germaine and make a line for Bond Street.'

Returning to the seclusion of her office, Fleur began to index and store away the strips of film which had been her task during the last months. It was hard and tedious work this hot morning, but she was glad of anything which

13

would help her come down to earth and collect her scattered thoughts into some semblance of order.

She made an effort to keep her mind from dwelling on the more glamorous and exotic part of the life which was spreading out in front of her. It would be full of gaiety and colour and all the sophisticated pleasures for which she had so often yearned in the past. But there was the other more practical side. She would have money. Lots of money with which she could help the family to enjoy those luxuries which they had never known.

The family! Fleur thought of her mother and sister. Poor darlings, they must learn to manage without her in the future. This was her big chance, and whatever else happened she must take it. If she made a success of her career she might soon be really rich, Mummy and Betty would be the first to benefit. Betty could leave the office where she worked as a typist, and take up the musical career which had always been her ambition. And Grandpa! Dear old Grandpa could buy himself all those textbooks over which he huddled in the public library, and might even be persuaded to order some new suits.

It was a decision which vitally concerned them all. A decision from which there could be no turning back. Their fate lay in the hands of the new Fleur Lorraine . . . Princess Fleur . . . who was determined that it should be sealed on the day the boat-train steamed out of Victoria station with a new-born star in the first-class Pullman-car.

CHAPTER TWO

Fleur sat on the sun-bathed terrace of the Café de Paris at Monte Carlo and for the tenth time that morning had to force herself to realise that the scene which lay around her was reality and not a dream.

For this town, it seemed to her, must surely be the culminating point in a series of unforgettable excitements. She saw a sea and sky of shimmering peacock blue, green palms amidst masses of vivid flowers, a fashionable crowd around the Casino gardens, little tables under gay striped umbrellas, the ornate villas and hotels and the general air of luxury and indolence. This was indeed the right setting for the fantastic existence which was now her life.

There had been weeks in London when, touring the West End dressmakers and milliners with Germaine in search of clothes and hats, she had enjoyed the novelty of being able to buy just what she wanted without having to haggle or worry over the price. There were visits to hairdressers and manicurists who, up till then, had only been famous names which one saw advertising in

15

the more expensive illustrated magazines. Antoine's—Raymond's—evening gowns by Molyneux, furs from Revillon, tailor-mades from Digby Morton—lovely, clever—original clothes designed for *her*. Often when she returned at the end of a long day to her home in Streatham Hill, there would be a silver box of orchids from Mark Manton, a case of champagne, or variety of perfumes with his card attached and a short formal message of good wishes.

'Cigarettes by Abdulla,' Betty laughed one evening, watching her sister open a parcel. 'It sounds like an advertisement in a theatre programme. Aren't you dazed?'

'Quite,' was Fleur's reply. But she kept her head, nevertheless.

At last the word came for which Fleur had waited. A telephone call from Mark Manton told her that everything was in order; they were booked to leave Victoria the day after tomorrow.

Fleur arrived at the station three-quarters of an hour before the train was due to leave, and walking up and down the platform kept looking anxiously towards the barrier for the first sign of Manton's arrival. It seemed an eternity before she saw him elbowing his way through the crowd. He came towards her ten minutes before the departure time, spruce and well-groomed in a heavy tweed travelling coat.

'Marvellous!' he exclaimed, taking her hand

16

and allowing his eyes to sweep over her with undisguised admiration. 'You look superb— those clothes are sure worthy of my princess.'

Fleur laughed happily. She knew that she was looking her best in that blue suit with platinum fox coat and ridiculous, chic little hat designed for her by Aage Thaarup.

'Fine feathers!' she smiled. 'The studio's cheque book and Germaine's taste, plus my own, are a pretty invincible combination.'

'I'll say they are,' Manton returned, leading her towards the Pullman-car. 'Sit down and order some coffee; I want to get you some papers.'

The selection of magazines which Manton bought Fleur remained unopened. The scene about her was more vivid than the most gripping short-story. She would never forget one moment of that journey all her life. She would remember the sleek grey destroyers which convoyed their crowded ship across the Channel and then turned swiftly towards Dover; the tense moment when they heard a dull crash and knew that depth-charges were being thrown overboard; the thrill of arriving at Boulogne harbour under the shadow of the monument which recorded the arrival of the first British troops in 1914, and seeing the first French *poilu* in his steel helmet and uniform. Outside the station a British military policeman controlled the traffic. It was war— war against Nazi Germany. Yet so far, thought

Fleur, it had been what they called the 'Bore War' and it had barely touched her life.

The Paris train was crowded, and seemed to stop at every station—stations whose names made Fleur's nerves tingle with the realisation that they were only a few miles from where the British and French Armies stood waiting for the attack which, it was rumoured, might be launched at any hour.

It was already dark when they steamed slowly past the suburbs into the Gare du Nord and Fleur had her fast view of wartime Paris. It was an experience which was to be engraved on her memory. As they walked down the platform by a buffet, where attractive white-coated girls served free *vin rouge* to a crowd of waiting soldiers, her first reaction was one of surprise at the amount of light which was to be seen. This was no blackout such as she had learned to know it in London. The shop windows glowed softly across comparatively well-lighted boulevards, along which taxis raced at an alarming speed.

'The French are a practical race,' Manton said, as they drove towards their hotel. 'When there's an *alerte* they merely switch off the street lights at the main.'

It was not until the next morning that Fleur, sitting in the café adjoining their hotel, saw that Paris was a city prepared and devoted to the war which might soon be fully unleashed against her with all a madman's fury.

There were uniforms on all sides. At the next table a group of officers sat laughing and drinking with a smartly dressed girl, who carried her gas-mask in a long tin container painted in the same pattern as the scarf around her neck. The eldest of the soldiers had three rows of ribbons across his chest and the round badge of the Maginot Line on his beret. Fleur could read the words: *'On ne passe pas'*.

'I wish we could stay here longer,' she said to Manton, who lounged beside her with a long cigar in his mouth. 'I've never known such a stimulating atmosphere. These people make one feel there is only one subject worth living for—one's country.'

'You won't be leaving the country,' Manton reminded her. 'You'll find the same atmosphere in the south.'

'I don't believe it. War has never really touched the Midi. The people here know they are living on the edge of a volcano which may erupt tomorrow.'

'What about Italy? Monte Carlo is practically a frontier town.'

Fleur gave an impatient little laugh.

'Italy! You don't expect me to take the Italians seriously. Gamelin says the French could be in Turin in three days.'

Shrugging his shoulders, Manton signed to the waiter for his bill. He did not want to discuss war or its consequences. He was not war-minded. The further he was away from any possible danger the better he would be pleased. The girl who was now his constant companion was his only serious thought. She filled his mind and body with a desire which was fast becoming a mania.

During the first days after they left Paris, Fleur lived in a trance of delight and youthful pleasure in her new state amidst the gay, carefree atmosphere of Monte Carlo. She found herself, indeed, living like a princess. Her suite on the first floor of the Hôtel de Paris was the finest that the management had to offer. Her windows faced the sea, and she knew all the exotic pleasure of the starlit nights when she could see the water shimmering in the moonlight and hear the soft music of the hotel orchestra wafted up to her room and watch the twinkling lights of the Casino.

Manton played the part of private secretary to perfection. He treated her with friendly attention and in public was most deferent. But Fleur realised that it was a part which he did not enjoy. She could sense that he was straining at the leash of friendship towards a more intimate relationship. She was afraid of him in that way, afraid lest he might spoil everything by making love to her.

They were constantly together, walking with the cosmopolitan crowd on the terrace, sitting outside cafés and hotels drinking their

20

morning apéritifs or lazing in the afternoon sunshine. At night they played in the roulette or baccarat rooms before walking across to the Café de Paris to dance.

Everywhere they went, people noticed Fleur, and it soon became rumoured publicly that the beautiful girl with the dark eyes and chestnut hair was a princess. Rumour whispered that she was as wealthy as she was lovely. Within a few days Fleur could not enter a restaurant or walk along the Boulevard des Moulins without being pointed out or talked about.

But Mark Manton was forgetting the real *raison d'être* for his presence here with Fleur. It was fast becoming apparent to him that he was desperately in love with Fleur, and that for the first time in his hard, egotistical career he had come in contact with a woman whom he wanted to have for his wife. Her beauty caught him by the throat and seemed to beat into his brain. His life was encircled by a picture of Fleur. Fleur in the most wonderful dresses; Fleur always cool and dignified and every inch a princess. Her self-possession amazed and angered him. Yes, he was amazed that she could play her part with such aplomb and confidence, and irritated because she never faltered from her attitude of grateful friendship towards him.

He knew that, for the moment, he dared not annoy or frighten her by amorous attentions.

First of all he must carry out the orders of his co-directors. Fleur Lorraine must be a household name before the moment could be chosen for the kidnapping stunt which was to be the crux of the whole publicity scheme.

This, Manton decided, was all for the best. The longer they remained in Monte Carlo the more certain it would be that Fleur would become inoculated with the romantic atmosphere of the place. He must play for time and wait for that moment of Mediterranean madness when her heart and body would rule her mind. Manton did not doubt that his moment would arrive. He knew what effect this languid southern climate with its artificially stimulated attractions had on the average man or woman.

For Fleur the days were all too short and wonderfully thrilling, and the world at Monte Carlo seemed to her a veritable if somewhat synthetic paradise. She sent home beautiful costly presents to the family. She felt she had tasted every good thing which life had to offer, that nothing was lacking to make her completely happy—until she met Blake Carew.

During the weeks which were to follow, Fleur often reflected on the caprice of fate which allowed her to fall wildly, deliriously and utterly in love with a man who was celebrated, not only on the Riviera, but in every capital and playground of Europe.

Her first impression on meeting Blake

Carew was of a man of about thirty-five, looking like a boy with his slim, athletic figure and handsome head, and that swift, graceful way he had of moving. She remembered noticing his brilliant, curiously light-grey eyes and short black lashes, his thick crisp hair and thin bronzed face. The most handsome man in Monte Carlo, people said, the gayest and most amusing and cynical.

There was little doubt that he was a confirmed cynic, believing in nobody, in nothing; skimming only the cream off life and finding it rather sour. He was obviously spoiled. But who was there to blame him? Men liked Blake Carew and women adored him in spite of the fact that he was sated with the choice things of life. They knew that he was in love with no woman and openly mocked at love.

It was on the evening of his return from a short Mediterranean cruise in his yacht that Blake, having climbed the long hill from Monaco harbour, strolled into the Casino and stared moodily at the tables where the usual crowds were gathered to play roulette.

His appearance in the gaming-rooms caused many heads to turn. The management and the more knowledgeable habitués knew that Blake Carew sometimes gambled heavily and with the most fantastic good luck.

'Money makes money,' they said. 'He doesn't care whether he wins or loses.'

23

But this time the crowd who hoped to watch some spectacular play were to be disappointed. The young English millionaire did not move towards the *Bureau de Change* but stood with his hands in the pockets of his dinner-jacket as though oblivious to his surroundings.

He did not seem to notice the many pretty women who sat or walked around the tables. There were some famous beauties. A dark-haired English actress, a famous dancer from the Russian Ballet, and the most glamorous of the American cabaret stars from Nice and Cannes. Women difficult for some men to win, but easy for Blake Carew with his youth, his good looks and his millions.

Tonight Blake was angry with life. Angry because he could so easily win money or the travesty which men called love. He felt restless and dissatisfied. He wanted the thrill of a chase, the excitement of reaching and striving for something which would be just outside his grasp.

Crossing the rooms towards a baccarat table, he stood watching the croupier flick out the cards from the wooden shoe. It was a small, uninteresting game, and he was on the point of leaving when suddenly the bored look in his eyes vanished as he found himself staring at the girl who sat at the middle of the table. A girl who was not playing but watching the cards which the man beside her held.

She was all in gold. A frock of gold lamé, tight-fitting to the hips, showing every curve of her slim figure, then flaring to the ankles. A gold cape lined with emerald-coloured chiffon lay across the back of her chair.

Blake liked the dress and liked, too, the fact that the girl wore no jewels. She was remarkable here in Monte for that fact. Still more did he like her vivid, eager face with the great dark eyes and flower-red mouth. Her hands—he was particular about hands—were perfect. Her fingers slender and white with almond, red-varnished nails.

He drew nearer to her, and Fleur, becoming suddenly conscious of his intense gaze, looked up to see a handsome young man with light grey eyes in a tired boyish face. For a moment the brilliant room seemed to spin around her. She felt a curious feeling of exhilaration as though she were being lifted up on a pinnacle far removed from the reality of her surroundings. Then a burning flush dyed her face and throat and she looked hastily towards Mark Manton and watched him stake his chips.

Blake Carew was delighted. It seemed years since he had seen a woman blush. He thought it enchanting, and walked up to a man he knew who was watching the game.

'Who is that girl in the gold dress?' he asked.

The man glanced towards Fleur.

'That is our latest celebrity—Princess Fleur.'

'Indeed,' said Blake. 'A princess, is she? One of these Balkan ladies, I suppose?'

'I imagine so. She has stacks of money, I'm told. Lives in a suite, at the Paris. She is always dressed marvellously.'

'And who is the boy friend?' Blake asked, indicating the hard-featured man who was talking with the girl as though he had known her all his life.

'The English secretary, Mark Manton. I spoke to him last night in the bar, as a matter of fact.'

'Then you can introduce me.'

They waited until the last cards in the shoe had been dealt, when Manton and Fleur pushed back their chairs and lit cigarettes. Then Fleur found herself shaking hands with Blake Carew. Just for a moment her hand lay in his, and just for a moment Blake's cynical eyes softened as they looked down into her face. He said:

'I am enchanted to meet you, Princess.'

Fleur murmured a suitable reply. Now that he was beside her she was amazingly conscious once again of that strange exhilaration, as though something, some vital spirit in this man, impelled and called to her. He kissed her hand. It was a light, formal touch, but it sent the blood coursing through her veins, and told her that, beyond doubt, she had fallen absurdly in love and at first sight.

It was Blake who suggested walking across to the Café de Paris for drinks, where they could get some of the fetid Casino air out of their lungs.

'Half an hour in "the Kitchen" is enough for me,' he said, when they were seated round a table overlooking the gardens. 'I call it a hell which has no boundaries.'

'And no limits!' said Manton grimly. 'I lost a packet tonight.'

'In that case we need champagne,' Blake smiled, signing to a waiter. 'Lots of champagne. If you have a sufficiently strong hangover in the morning it takes your mind off the night's losses.'

Sitting back in her chair, Fleur tried to concentrate on the frivolous conversation which went on around her. But it was of no avail. She felt absurdly self-conscious and tongue-tied, as though she had no control over her faculties. Manton noticed it and gave her a warning look. She was not acting the part of the sophisticated princess tonight. Probably, he decided, she was tired, in which case it would be safer to break up the party.

'I think we should be moving along,' he said, draining his third glass of champagne. 'The Princess is tired. She has had a long day.'

Fleur felt almost relieved when Blake got to his feet and putting her cloak around her shoulders, said:

'I agree. Late hours are the curse of this place.'

Putting out her hand, Fleur tried to control her voice when she spoke.

'I'm afraid I have been very dull. The heat in the Casino always makes me sleepy. But there's no reason for Mark to leave. I can easily walk across the Camembert by myself.'

Her words spurred Manton to greater haste. Taking her arm, he shook hands with Blake and his friend.

'I'm tired myself. Thanks for the drink, Carew.'

Fleur could sense the fact that Manton was displeased with her, but she did not broach the subject until they were back in their suite in the hotel. Then, sitting down in a chair, she took a cigarette from a box on the table beside her.

'I behaved badly tonight, Mark. I'm sorry.'

'That's all right,' he replied, flicking open a gold lighter. 'I could see you were tired, so I thought it better to get going. Blake Carew could be a useful cog in our wheel, if we played our cards properly.'

The colour flamed in Fleur's cheeks.

'What do you mean?'

'Just what I say. He could be useful. Carew is a celebrity here. He is front page news, and there's no reason why he shouldn't take you on to the headlines with him.'

Fleur pressed out her cigarette with an

28

angry gesture.

'There's nothing in my contract to the effect that I should run after men.'

Manton gave a short laugh.

'You can take it from me,' he said unpleasantly, 'that you won't have to do much of the running. From what I hear about Carew, he will be hanging around here before you know where you are.'

'You're speaking through that champagne, Mark,' Fleur returned coldly. 'You should know better than listen to Riviera gossip.'

'I'm merely telling you I think the man is a bounder.'

'And I tell you I think him charming.'

Manton looked up hastily to see angry light in her eyes. A light which warned him that he was treading on dangerous ground. He knew the attraction which Carew held over women, and cursed the chance which had thrown him in their way. If there seemed any likelihood of Fleur failing for this man, the publicity part of it could go to the devil. Fleur was his first and only consideration.

Sitting down on the arm of her chair, he tried to control his temper. The fragrance of her so near him, and the slim, proud young figure close to his, went like wine to his head. He put a hand on her knee.

'Don't misunderstand me, my dear,' he said earnestly. 'I am the last person to want you to chuck yourself at any man's head. I want to

29

keep you for myself. Can't you see what I mean? How I feel? Can't you see that I'm crazy about you? Tell me . . .'

Pushing his hand away, Fleur jumped to her feet. The dreaded moment had come and she hardened her heart to deal with it. She knew Mark now. She saw no reason to be soft with *him*. He could take care of himself.

'Don't be a fool, Mark,' she returned. 'We came here together on business terms. I'm carrying out my share of the contract. I expect you to do the same.'

'You mean platonic friendship is enough for you?'

She looked him straight in the eyes.

'I mean it is all there can ever be between us, Mark. I am eternally grateful for your help, for the chance you gave me. That is why I must be frank with you. It's kinder to tell you now.'

Manton gave a deprecating shrug of his shoulders.

'That is what you say tonight, my dear. You're tired—overwrought. The excitement of the last few weeks has upset your mental balance. But it will readjust itself. I'm content to wait for that moment.'

Fleur did not reply. Picking up her cloak and bag, she walked from the room and a moment later Manton heard her bedroom door shut and the click of a key turning in the lock.

For some minutes the man stood staring

moodily in front of him, his heavy face flushed and angry. Then, pouring out a stiff whisky-and-soda, he crossed to the window and looked down upon the flood-lit gardens.

'To hell with Blake Carew!' he murmured thickly. 'Blast his millions, and his party manners—and his youth! If he gets dangerous, we'll finish off this publicity stunt. We'll go back to England. I want Fleur Lorraine for myself—and I mean to get her.'

CHAPTER THREE

At eleven o'clock the next morning Blake Carew ran up the stairs of the Hôtel de Paris, acknowledged the salute of the bemedalled Senegalese doorman with a wave of his hand, and walking to the reception-office, asked to be put through on the telephone to Princess Fleur's suite.

A moment later he heard the sound of the receiver being raised, and Manton's voice answered him. The secretary sounded disgruntled.

'The Princess is busy. She doesn't want to be disturbed.'

Blake was not accustomed to a peremptory dismissal.

'It's Blake Carew speaking. I only want a word with her.'

31

'Sorry, Carew.' The voice was frankly hostile now. 'I'm repeating what the Princess told me.' The receiver was returned to its cradle with a crack which echoed in Blake's ear. Slowly he turned towards the lounge, an amused smile on his face.

'Surly devil,' he thought. 'His hangover must be a good 'un.'

But this morning no man's alcoholic remorse was of any interest to Blake. Everything, apart from the ever-present nightmare of the European war, seemed for the best in the best of possible worlds. For since last night he knew that he had met the one woman who could change his personal life from a monotonous, meaningless round; a woman with whom he could soar to a cloudless and ever-blue sky which would know no limit. Last night, when he stood outside the Café de Paris watching the back of her chestnut head as she walked across the Camembert, the realisation had come to him that there was a girl who could make him more than ever conscious of the futility of the aimless existence which so many of the men and women with whom he came in contact called life. Even now—with Europe at war—such men and women existed.

Setting himself on a red plush settee in the lounge, he called a waiter.

'*A quart de Vichy* and the *Petit Niçois.*'

The concierge who brought the paper

looked worried.

'The news is not good, *monsieur*. The Germans have broken the Belgian defences near Maastricht. The bridges at Sedan were not blown up. *Que faire?* These *sacrés* tanks have it all their own way.'

Blake glanced down the daily communiqué which he was learning to dread. Its anaemic phraseology made him hunger for a realistic description of what was taking place in the north. He had a sickly, uneasy presentiment that the French were employing wild and desperate tactics in an attempt to conceal the truth from the country.

'*Our forces,*' (he read), '*have withdrawn in order to re-establish the continuity of the line. The situation is serious but not critical.*'

Throwing down the paper, Blake sipped his drink and looked around him. The lounge of the hotel was filling up with the same careless, chattering crowd who were in the Casino last night and who would be in it again tonight. It was the same self-centred crowd whom he had known in every playground of Europe. In the days of peace he had found them negative but harmlessly amusing. Now he wanted to stand up and ask them if they were incapable of realising that the country which sheltered and fed them was fighting for its very existence.

Was it possible that they were content to live in a synthetic fool's paradise, when the country's army was in the midst of a retreat which was reaching a momentum of sixty miles a day? Could they still react to the syncopated fiddling of the hotel's *chef d'orchestre* while Lille burned? Could their consciences really be at rest when all they did for the war-effort was to buy tickets for some charity concert or spend money at the weekly gala dinner in aid of *Les Mutilés de la Guerre*? His only comfort when he watched them throwing away their money in the Casino was the fact that the Government took a good sixty per cent of the syndicate's winnings for themselves.

Blake's train of thought was broken when the lift door opened and Fleur walked out of the shadows towards the sunlit terrace.

He rose and bowed, throwing away his half-smoked cigarette.

'Princess,' he said, standing before her. 'You must forgive me if I appear impudent. Your secretary did not sound too pleased when I suggested calling so I decided to stay around until you arrived.'

Fleur made an effort to appear unconcerned by the fact that any man should settle down to wait for her. But her pulses were leaping as she looked into the grey, attractive eyes of Blake Carew again. And she could not conceal a smile when he spoke of Manton. She had heard Mark's words as he answered the telephone in their suite, and had listened to a tirade against Blake.

'Insolent young swine!' Mark had grumbled.

'Thinks his money is a pass-key to your room. Spoke to me as though I were a blasted servant.'

The very fact that she wanted to be with Blake prompted Fleur to show him that she was unlike the other women who ran after him. She had made up her mind to treat him with a coolness which she was far from feeling.

She said lightly:

'My secretary is not very well this morning. I hope he was not too curt with you.'

Blake laughed.

'I'm afraid his tone didn't worry me. I was only interested in seeing you.'

Fleur looked at him. She felt incapable of exchanging banal platitudes with this man. He was so gloriously insolent and sure of himself, standing there in his perfectly cut grey suit, his boyish head flung back and his keen eyes challenging her.

'Why did you want to see me?'

'To ask if I may take you to any café you may choose for an apéritif.'

Fleur did not hesitate. She knew that if she stayed here in the hotel it would mean spending the morning with Mark, who, in his present mood, was the last person she wanted to see.

She answered Blake softly.

'I should love to go with you.'

A moment later she was ready to go out with him in all the perfection of her white tailored suit with jade green trimming, big linen white hat, jade green scarf—exquisite sandals on bare, sun-browned feet, a big green bag. The princess-of-fashion, of loveliness complete, and enough to go like wine to Blake Carew's head.

They spent an enchanting morning sitting in the sun at a little table under a red-and-white awning, where they drank iced coffee and looked at the multicoloured flowers, the sophisticated crowd, listened to an American dance band. They were happy. Fleur gloriously so. Blake curiously. He had known almost all the thrills which his world had to offer and had grown bored. But sitting with, talking to, this girl, he was content. Princess—or commoner; she was the only woman he had ever known who had ever really charmed him.

He discovered that she was extraordinarily simple and unspoiled, and that it was absurdly easy to bring that fascinating colour to her cheeks. He learned that she was staying in Monte Carlo with her secretary for an indefinite period. Of her home and her past she said nothing, and he stopped questioning her when he found that she did not seem to wish to talk about that part of her life. When he mentioned the perfection of the English which she spoke, she explained that she had been educated in a famous English girls' school.

The things she told Blake were lies which

had been prompted by Manton. Mark impressed upon her the fact that they must be sure to stick to the same story. The lies at first seemed amusing and of no importance to Fleur. But somehow, when she repeated them to Blake, they assumed a magnitude which depressed and worried her. She hated to look into those grey, penetrating eyes of his and reel off a list of romantic fabrications. But it had to be done. Nobody in Monte Carlo, least of all the famous Blake Carew, must guess the truth.

She spoke of England.

'I often long for London,' she said. 'I love this place with all its warmth and beauty—I have been wonderfully happy since I arrived— but that very happiness makes me feel selfish during wartime.'

Leaning towards her, Blake put a hand on her arm.

'I'm glad you said that,' he said, with undisguised satisfaction in his voice. 'It's a pity more of these people don't think along the same lines. Can you imagine how I feel sitting around here doing nothing? I had a destroyer until I got pneumonia at Scapa last winter, and a medical-board threw me out on my ear. Some damn' silly verdict that my heart was wonky. You could hardly believe it, could you?'

'I certainly couldn't to look at you,' she smiled. 'But sun-tan can be deceptive.'

'Oh, I'm O.K. so long as I don't dance more

than one in three,' he smiled back, 'or rush upstairs, and in time they say I'll recover. Then I'll have another shot for the Navy.'

His words removed the last vestige of doubt which she had held about him. When Mark told her about Blake's reputation—that he despised women because he won them so easily—she had been mildly scornful. But the suggestion that the millionaire-Englishman was a pacifist—a conscientious objector who should be in uniform instead of leading an aimless life on the Riviera, had rankled in her mind. Now she knew that Mark's story was untrue. She believed every word that Blake Carew said.

She knew that Blake was everything which she could want a man to be. He had been in the Navy and discharged on account of health. He was amusing and attractive. He had seen and done much. He had an endless store of anecdotes to interest her and was a born raconteur. Utterly different from any man she had met in her life before. Not that there had ever been any particular man in Fleur's life. She had thought of love and what it could mean, but until last night, when she first saw Blake Carew in the Casino, she had been disinterested in men and smugly wrapped up in the excitement of her publicity stunt and future career.

At the end of the morning, when Blake walked back with her to her hotel, he on his part was more than ever intrigued. This mysterious princess was so very beautiful, so simple and not in the slightest degree blasé. Yet at the same time there was a subtle aloofness, a reserve in Fleur which attracted him vitally. She was a strange mixture of simplicity and sophistication. There were moments when it seemed to him that she almost resented his presence and others when she hung on his every word. His invitations to sail on his yacht, to motor with him in his sports Delage, or dine with him at the Sporting Club, seemed to both please and frighten her.

When they parted she was still courteous but detached. At the door of the hotel he took her hand and looked at her with frank perplexity in his eyes. This girl baffled and eluded him. He felt instinctively that she was holding something back which she was timid of revealing. He did not know what it was, and he did not really care. He only knew that he had fallen crazily, headlong in love, and that she was the only woman in the world he would like for his wife. Yes, Blake Carew—confirmed bachelor—had at last met the one and only being whom he wished to marry.

He returned to his yacht glowing with thoughts of his princess, of her loveliness, her adorable pride and sudden reservation, her grace and dignity.

'Every inch a princess,' he thought, 'and the one wife for Blake Carew. I shall win that girl or die in the attempt. I adore her. I will break down that strange barrier of reserve. There is fire under the snow and I shall find it.'

For Fleur, that morning was the prelude to strange, exciting and perilous days—days in which the hours seemed to race by on gilt-edged wings. Days during which it often seemed to her that she must be in a dream. Only when she remembered that there could not be many more days of this sunlit beauty and romance in Monte Carlo, and that her role of princess must soon end, came a sinking feeling in her heart.

Mark Manton was communicating with London to make final arrangements for the kidnapping plot. And when that was over—everything else would be over too.

Blake followed Fleur wherever she went. She tried to avoid him, knowing at the same time that she wanted to see him. She tried to feel angry when she found him waiting in her hotel, and could not. She could only feel a maddening thrill of pleasure and happiness which drowned her saner moments. Moments when she realised that every fresh meeting with him must make the ultimate parting more painful. His dogged devotion wore down her every resolution, until she reached a state when she grew almost faint with rapture at the sight of the tall, graceful figure—the bronzed, handsome face with the gay, cynical eyes—this Blake, late Lieutenant-Commander of the

R.N.V.R.

Each morning he sent flowers to her suite, boxes of mimosa, roses, carnations, orchids. All the loveliest, most extravagant flowers in the south of France filled the 'Princess's' suite. The staff of the hotel began to speak of this new and obvious romance which was taking place under their roof, and of the tips which they were welcoming from the journalists who came in search of news.

The local paper was the first to publish the story which was common gossip. It was printed on the front page under a photograph of *'Balkan Princess and Mr. Blake Carew on the Casino terrace'*, and was the first of a series of articles which pleased and angered Manton. The publicity was what he had come to France for. If only Blake had not been implicated, it would have been perfect. Manton's one consolation was that they would soon be able to return to England.

Blake was frankly and audaciously pleased that his name was being linked with Fleur's. He loved her desperately. One day the world would know that this sweet, brown-eyed princess was his own. He had his millions to lay at her feet. Her title, he reflected gaily, would please his various relatives and friends who wanted him to marry well. He had done some reckless and graceless things, but not even his most snobbish aunt could upbraid him for marrying a princess.

For Fleur the sudden outbursts of publicity meant the end of her romantic dreams. By now she found it impossible to avoid Blake or still the frantic throbbing of her heart when he came near her. The time had come for her to end it all—and end it quickly. She loved him too deeply to risk hurting his name or his heart. She must make a complete break before it was too late.

There were moments when she wondered whether she should tell him the truth—that she was an impostor working up a publicity stunt. She could not break the promise in her contract. Blake might believe and forgive her but she dare not run the risk. It would probably mean the loss of the two things which meant everything to her—the man she loved *and* her career. There was only one thing to do. She must go on lying to Blake—and act a new, devastating part as she had never acted the other. She must seize the first possible opportunity to convince him that love and marriage meant nothing to her.

The moment which she wanted and dreaded came one warm, starlit night when they were dancing in the ballroom of the hotel. Blake had given a small party to which, out of sheer courtesy, he had been forced to ask Mark Manton, the secretary. He did not want Manton in his present state of morose hostility. But he invited an attractive young Frenchwoman to go with them in the hope that

42

she might be able to amuse Mark. The attempt proved a failure. Manton avoided the French girl. His attention was never diverted from Fleur. All evening he had followed her every movement with unconcealed jealousy.

Blake was irritated but unconcerned. It was sufficient for him to know that he was near Fleur, to be able to talk and look at her.

He thought that he had never seen her look more bewitchingly lovely than she did tonight. A dress of white slipper-satin, divinely cut by Lanvin, clung tightly to her slim figure. There was a great spray of pinkish orchids at her shoulder (orchids Blake had sent). Two ropes of pearls around her neck; ruby and diamond bracelets glittering on her arms. She attracted an enormous amount of attention. Men looked at her glorious young figure. Women at her dress, her jewels, her mink coat, the queenly little head of chestnut curls, sculptured by Antoine. The ruby studs in her small ears.

Blake's arm held her tightly when they danced. He found her light, fragrant and easy to guide over the crowded floor. He had eyes for nobody else. He could not take them from the beautiful, vivid little face. Touching her orchids, he said:

'You are wearing my flowers.'

She nodded.

'I always wear orchids with white satin.'

He gave a short excited laugh.

'When I send flowers to a lovely lady I

expect her to wear them because I gave them to her.'

'Ah, but you are spoiled, *mon ami*.'

He looked at her curiously. Her voice sounded almost hard, yet her eyes were exquisitely soft and he could feel her tremble slightly in his arms.

He said:

'You don't spoil me, my dear. I wish to God you would. There are times when you are frankly unkind.'

'Every man tells me that.'

Blake's eyes grew less cynical and more fiercely honest than she had ever seen them.

'Princess,' he said in a low voice, 'all my life I have been spoiled. You are right. I have got what I wanted. I mean to get what I want *now*.'

Her brows lifted.

'And that is?'

'You. You in white satin—a bridal satin with which you would wear the orange blossoms of the South, and a veil of Mechlin lace.'

A small pulse throbbed in Fleur's throat. For a moment she thought that she could not go on, that her legs must give way under her. Then she realised with relief that the band had stopped playing. With a superhuman effort she smiled at Blake and made her way through the crowd, towards an open french window which led on to the terrace. He followed and stood beside her as she reached the balustrade. She gripped the stone rails with shaking hands and stared with blind eyes towards the glitter of the lights below.

The knowledge that the next minutes would send her hurling over the edge of the world of love which had grown up around her was like cold steel in her heart. She wondered with acute misery how it was possible to love anybody so much as she loved this marvellous man. So intensely was she aware of his nearness that it left her breathless and weak. She knew that he was waiting for her to speak, to give him her answer. When she turned towards him she had forced another casual smile to her lips.

'You talk like a romantic boy, Blake Carew. And I thought you were the complete cynic.'

There was no answering smile in his eyes when they met hers.

'A cynic is an inverted idealist. I happen to have found the ideal woman. I mean to have her.'

Shrugging her shoulders, Fleur took a cigarette from her case and struck a match.

'You surprise me, my dear. We've had a lot of fun. I've thoroughly enjoyed it. But you must surely realise that the difference between our social positions is insurmountable.'

'You mean that because you are of royal blood I am not good enough for you?'

'If you must put it that way—I do.'

There was a long pause during which Fleur felt rather than saw the look of pained

45

astonishment which spread across Blake's face. She knew that her words had hurt him deeply, that he was striving to regain his mental balance before he replied. She saw that his whole face had changed. His eyes had narrowed, his mouth had grown grim. When he spoke, his voice was brittle.

'It might have been better to point all this out to me before the papers made us front page news. Apart from any feelings I might possibly have had, I wonder that you allowed your name to be so publicly linked with mine if you felt that I was *presuming*—and not entitled to ask you to marry me.'

Fleur turned away her head so that she could not see the expression in his eyes.

'Yes, perhaps I should have warned you before, but I did not want to hurt you. I liked you—your friendship so much.'

Blake threw back his head and laughed. It was a humourless laugh which almost shook her resolve to continue with this farce, whether she let down her employers and the film studio or not.

'My poor, proud little Princess,' said Blake, turning towards the ballroom, 'at times you are almost human. Let me take you back to our table before any of those reporters find us out here alone. After that you need not worry. The family escutcheon is in no further danger of being tainted by the proletariat.'

Speechless, white to the lips, Fleur turned

and walked back into the hotel.

Blake was still laughing when they reached their table and sat down beside Manton. The secretary looked at them both with mistrust.

'You've been away a long time,' he said. 'If you study those stars much more often, you will be turning into astrologists.'

Pouring out a glass of champagne, Blake drank it down and leaned back in his chair.

'I didn't notice the stars tonight,' he said slowly. 'As a matter of fact, the Princess was giving me an interesting talk on court etiquette. I never realised how much there was to learn. No, I didn't see the stars. Why don't you take her out and make sure they are still there?'

CHAPTER FOUR

Mark Manton put down the copy of the *Continental Daily Mail* which he had been reading, with every appearance of gloom, and studied the ash on the end of his long cigar.

This trip to Monte Carlo, he reflected grimly, had not turned out to be the carefree, romantic interlude for which he had hoped and planned. Blake Carew was, of course, the deepest thorn in his flesh. It had been the devil's own luck that Fleur had ever met him. But he had to admit that the fellow had been

47

gratifyingly conspicuous by his absence since the party at the beginning of the week.

The young millionaire had acted strangely during the latter part of that evening. He had drunk much more than usual. His conversation had been unusually flippant and artificial. His manners and behaviour had been almost studiously correct, but he had said good night to them in the lounge of the hotel and not been back since. It was almost as though he had quarrelled with Fleur, but when Manton had sounded Fleur on the subject, he had been unable to glean any information from her. Her answers were not only non-committal; the very mention of Blake's name was sufficient to make her more than usually terse with him. Manton guessed there had been trouble, and it infuriated him to find her so secretive about it. Nevertheless he was relieved that Blake Carew was 'out of it'.

Now the war news, which was splashed across the papers in huge headlines and shouted from every radio, plunged Mark further into an ever-growing well of fear and despondency. No longer could the most carefully worded communiqué hide the fact that France and her Empire were in danger. The Germans were advancing from the north in a seemingly endless swarm. Weygand had taken the place of Gamelin, the 'philosopher soldier'. Mussolini was making a series of bombastic speeches in which he threatened that the moment was approaching for the Fascist sword to be drawn from the scabbard.

The news caused undisguised consternation among the *hôteliers* and shopkeepers, who saw their livelihood being taken from them. Every day Manton watched a flow of visitors and residents leaving for England. On enquiring at the station, he was told by a harassed official that every *wagon-lit* was reserved for six weeks ahead. Manton cursed. The idea of sitting up at night in an overcrowded train did not appeal to him, but he had made up his mind that he and Fleur had better get out of the country at the first possible moment. Mark liked the luxuries of life, but he was also a coward. He was afraid to stay in France. They must go if it meant travelling in a cattle-truck. He felt thankful that everything at last was arranged for the final episode his publicity scheme. Nothing—not Mussolini himself—should stop that.

That evening Mark explained to Fleur the details of the plan which he had worked out. She sat at the far end of her reception-room, turning over the pages of *Marie Claire*. On Sunday night there was to be a gala dinner and dance in the hotel, so it was advertised, in aid of the Croix Rouge.

Mark had arranged for the actual kidnapping to take place in the gardens during the dance. Fleur would be with a partner who knew nothing about the affair. Three men would carry her off. Her partner would naturally raise the alarm, after which she need only lie low for a day or two in quarters which he had taken some miles down the coast. They would then return to England.

'And after that,' Manton concluded, 'Balham and the studios, and Fleur Lorraine's name ringing through England and France.'

Fleur gave a brief laugh.

'Coupled with the world-shaking news that Italy may at any moment march into France, a big chance there is now of *my* publicity being got over!'

Manton looked at her resentfully. She had treated him unmercifully during the last few days. He would be really thankful when the 'Princess' business was over. Once she was just Fleur Lorraine, working under his personal direction in the studio, things would be very different. As for this war-hysteria, it would die down, he thought. But the films would go on.

Throwing a coat around her shoulders, Fleur left the room and walked down the stairs towards the entrance to the hotel gardens. Manton's presence was more than she could bear in her present state of dejection. She knew that he was aware of some mysterious trouble between Blake Carew and herself, and that Mark was still hoping for some response from her. Perhaps, she thought, he suspected a lover's quarrel and hoped to win her on the rebound.

At any other time the idea would have amused her. But now she was too frankly miserable to find it funny. There was only one man who could ever mean anything in her life. Blake, whom she might never see again, and without whom she wondered if she could ever carry on with her life. It was so terrible to her to know that he despised her now; regarded her as a proud, snobbish twopenny-half-penny Balkan princess who thought herself too superior to stoop to him. To *him* whom she adored! Dear God, she thought, if only he knew how small and insignificant Fleur Lorraine really was! If only she could *explain.*

Wandering into the gardens, she crossed the terrace and sat down on a marble slab overlooking the sea. Behind her a mass of dark ilexes and cypress trees showed up the white of her linen dress, She never knew how long she had been there, when she saw the tall figure of a man come swiftly across the lawn towards her. For a moment she wondered if her tired brain was playing tricks with her. This man might have been a young god, a creature of the moon with his pale, ardent face, his dark head magnificently poised. He wore a white yachting suit and was hatless. Raising her eyes, Fleur looked into his face. The blood rushed to her cheeks and she gained her feet slowly, uncertainly.

'Blake!'

For a moment he did not speak. She could

see his lips working, the intense ardour in his eyes. Then he said:

'I have been everywhere—everywhere to try and find you. Manton said you were in your room. I knew he was lying. I hunted until I found you.'

'It was wrong of you to come.'

He raised a hand as though to stop her words.

'Don't tell me what is right or wrong. I had to come. I had to see you.'

'Why?'

'You know why.'

The colour remained in her cheeks, burning red. Her dark eyes fell before his.

'How should I know?' she said, trying to control her voice.

'You know that you didn't mean what you said the other night. Neither of us meant what we said. We were both keyed up—hysterical. I've been half mad since, and sorry that I was bitter and angry. I regret any superficial boasts I ever made to you. I regret any woman to whom I ever paid futile compliments, or looked at—before you came into my life.'

'I don't want you to have any regrets,' she said, and put a hand to her lips to stop their quivering. This torrent of words from Blake dazed her. She was still dazed when he suddenly caught her hand and pulled it away from her mouth.

'Please,' he said hoarsely, 'don't cover that

52

adorable mouth, Fleur.'

It was the first time he had spoken her name. Always before he had called her 'Princess'. It was sheer heaven to hear him say it. She *was* Fleur—and she loved him. Pride, rebellion, the fear of being despised were forgotten. He was kissing her hand, dropping kisses on the smooth palm. In that moment he seemed to her like the god of love himself, his handsome face pale and passionate in the moonlight. To Fleur he *was* a god, and she had suddenly become a goddess. This was their pagan garden of glamorous love. She looked at him through half-shut lids, her breath coming fast.

'Give me time to think, Blake,' she whispered.

He looked down at her, his face both suppliant and masterful.

'Don't waste time thinking, my adorable Fleur; I love you. You need only think of that.'

She shut her eyes, She was weak with the surge of emotion which he roused in her. The moonlit world was spinning crazily about her. She said:

'I know you love me.'

'Then look at me, Fleur. Tell me that you are going to love me—that you will let me love you. You are a princess but you are a woman—an adorable woman made for me.'

'Blake,' she whispered. 'Oh—*darling!*'

He knew then that he had won. The next

moment the sweet warmth of her body was in his arms. He was kissing her hair, her cheeks, her throat. When he came to her lips he paused for a moment and said:

'Look at me before I kiss your mouth. Look at me and say "I love you" . . .'

Her lashes lifted. Trembling in his arms, she looked up at him and knew that the prospect of death itself could not make her lie to him now.

'I love you, Blake.'

His lips covered hers and clung in a kiss so intense that time and space were no more. The world of jewelled stars and shimmering moonlight and the scent of a thousand flowers were forgotten.

'My sweet,' he murmured against her ear, 'my own sweet love. Tell me that I have found not only a princess, but the girl who will be my wife.'

She stood quite still, looking towards the sea as though she did not dare to formulate her thoughts. Her face was no longer warmly red. It was pale, and seemed to him almost ethereal in the starlight, with those great dark eyes under the shadowy curtains of their lashes. She hung back in his arms, breathing deeply. She remembered the lies which she had told him on the night of the dance; on so many other days. How would he react if she told him now that she was no princess, that she had no blue blood in her veins, no money?

That she was just a would-be film actress striving for publicity? Could any man's love stand for that? Would any man want to marry a woman who had deliberately fed him for weeks on an ever growing pack of lies? Could he ever be expected to honour or trust her again?

They had been god and goddess in their ecstasy, but now, she thought, with a new stab of pain, they were man and woman; ordinary human beings with very ordinary human reactions.

Slipping from his arms, she drew a hand across her eyes.

'You must let me go, Blake. I can't answer you now.'

'Why not? he asked impatiently. 'You love me. You *must* answer me tonight.'

She shook her head.

'Tomorrow, please.'

He was disappointed. Frowning, he looked for a moment with sudden attentiveness into the deep mist of her eyes. When he spoke, his voice held a note of mild surprise.

'Very well, my sweet, let it be tomorrow if you wish it. I can only say, once again, that I adore you; that I offer you my love and anything I may possess. It may not be good enough for a princess—but all that I have is yours.'

Her eyes filled with tears. She felt that this false position, the lies and the knowledge that lay in her heart, were suffocating. She must go. She must get away where she could think what to say—and what to do.

'Thank you, dearest Blake,' she said. 'You are very kind and understanding. You deserve the happiness of a perfect love.'

'Then give me yours, my darling. Good night—and God bless you.'

She walked quickly away.

Long after she had left, Blake Carew sat on the stone seat and held the thought of her to his heart. He would always treasure the memory of those responsive lips and clinging arms. His Fleur! His princess—the first and only woman to make him care! He built up an ideal about her, set her on a pedestal and adored her.

His reflections on this dazzling new love which had come into his life were broken by the appearance of two men who came quietly across the lawn from the direction of the hotel. As they passed, the moon slipped behind a cloud, leaving Blake's figure in shadow. The men stood by a cypress tree, talking and smoking. Blake could not see their faces, but he recognised the slow voice of one. Manton. Fleur's secretary whom he had grown to dislike. He detested the man's possessive attitude towards Fleur. His studied cunning. Most of all he hated the way Manton cringed. There was nothing manly or courageous about him.

'The sooner I get out of this place, George,' he heard Manton's voice, 'the better I'll be pleased. The news is worse. There's a rumour going about that Leopold may capitulate.'

The man addressed as George gave a short laugh.

'Nonsense, my dear Mark. Leopold is the reincarnation of his father. The Belgians say his patriotism is only equalled by his courage.'

'I don't give a damn what they say. I don't trust that curly-headed darling. If he throws in the sponge, we'll be in a pretty mess.'

'We certainly will. The B.E.F. cut off; the road to Dunkirk closed. It doesn't bear thinking about.'

'No, but I'm thinking about myself,' came Manton's terse reply. 'I have no wish to be stranded here and chucked into a concentration camp for the duration. I have a perfectly good flat waiting for me in Bruton Street. I promise you that after the Sunday business is finished with, you won't see me for dust.'

Blake felt a sudden wave of nausea spread over him as he listened to the secretary's words. He half rose to his feet. He wanted to face Manton and tell him what he thought of his lack of patriotism—his cowardice—his thorough egotism in the teeth of war of such magnitude. He yearned to tell him to keep his defeatist talk to himself. Then he paused. He heard a sentence which held him back.

Curiosity and suspicion overcame mere apathy.

'It's all fixed for Sunday, is it?' the man named George asked Manton.

'Everything,' was Manton's answer. 'I'd like to see some of the people's faces round here when they learn that the famous Princess Fleur is a jumped-up little actress in the pay of Filmograph Limited.

'How does your scheme work?'

'Perfectly simple,' Manton replied. 'You and the boys will grab her at nine-thirty in these gardens. Say at this spot. I've arranged with her to bring her unsuspecting partner here. Then you merely take her in the car along the coast to the château. She'll stay hidden there until I get her quickly to London while the police are still hunting for her. It'll be the best publicity stunt of the year.'

'And then?'

'Then the producer can get on with the film, and I can get on with my wedding.'

'You're getting married?'

'Sure, I am. To Fleur. I'm crazy about her. It was I who was instrumental in bringing her out here. When we get home she's going to give me my reward. She's been fooling around with young Carew, but there's a big laugh coming *his* way when he finds that Her Highness is just an ordinary little English girl, Miss Fleur Lorraine, of Streatham Hill.'

Blake heard the voices die away. Manton

and his friend had gone.

For some time Blake sat like a figure of stone, staring out to sea. The bottom had fallen out of his world—a world which, some minutes before, had seemed full of endless promise.

So *this* was the truth! Fleur was a fake. Her whole association with him had been built up out of a tissue of lies. She was no princess. Just a cheat. A Miss Lorraine of Streatham Hill working up a publicity stunt, and going to marry Manton. The girl whom he had openly worshipped and believed in was an actress— and a damned good one, he thought bitterly. She had taken him in, as well as the whole of Monte Carlo.

The thought made him writhe with sheer pain. His was the agony of hurt love mingled with wounded vanity. Blake had really loved Fleur. He had given her the deepest, the best in him, and offered her his life's service. But all that dignity, that shy, reserved manner of his 'Princess' had been pose. She had done nothing but pose, day after day, night after night. Tonight, when she let him kiss her and pour out his heart's passion, she must have been secretly laughing at him, he reflected grimly.

Blake's grey eyes grew flint-like. The boyish mouth took on its old stern, cynical curve. So much for romance and ideals, he thought! Life had played a nasty trick on him, but he wasn't finished with it yet. Not by a long way. He did not intend to sit down placidly and watch Manton and his friends jeer at him. No, he told himself, savagely, there was another and better way out. He would beat them all at their own game—and beat Fleur at hers.

His feelings about her had changed in the revelation of this hour. Idealism, worship, gave place to anger and contempt.

'Wait, my dear Princess,' he said softly aloud. 'Wait until Sunday. You came out here for publicity. Well, you shall have it. I shall help you to get it, my dear little Miss Lorraine, in no uncertain fashion.'

CHAPTER FIVE

The gala dinner and dance in the Hôtel de Paris was generally a success, in spite of an obvious thinning out of the more regular patrons in these uneasy days of war. Those people who were left appeared to throw themselves into the festivities with more than usual abandon, as though they feared that it might be the last ball to be held in the hotel before it finally shut its doors.

These men and women—of all nationalities—knew that they were drinking and dancing on the eve of a disaster which was to rock Europe and the world. The rumour about Leopold had become fact. *'Le Roi Félon'* had capitulated to the invader, leaving the British Army isolated in Flanders. Mr. Churchill had warned his country to expect hard and heavy tidings. It seemed probable that many of the British residents on the Riviera would be unable to leave France. The habitués of the Casino realised that the next days would be a gamble with the odds against them. There was nothing to do except wait—and trust in Weygand.

To Fleur the evening was a nightmare. The man whom Manton had selected for her partner was an added source of irritation. He had been introduced to her as Count Delbos. He was a tall, spare Frenchman, who spent his time paying her fatuous compliments which she scarcely heard. She was in a state bordering on panic, and her whole body throbbing with excitement and nerves.

Under the excitement was intense worry and distress. Since her last meeting with Blake she had never ceased worrying as to what she should say to him. At last she had decided to tell him the truth with her own lips. She could not go on deceiving him. But when she telephoned it was only to be told by his valet that Blake was away on business.

He appeared to have left Monte Carlo on the morning following their love-scene in the garden.

It seemed queer to her that he should have

left the place so suddenly. Still stranger that she had received no word from him. No farewell message. Not even a bunch of flowers. Nor a reminder of their first enthralling hour of love, and of the answer he awaited. What had happened? she wondered uneasily. Would he come back? Had he gone for good; run away from her and her love?

She was disheartened and afraid as the hour for the carrying out of Manton's plan approached. There was no way of communicating with Blake. She had to go through with her detested role. So it meant the end. The end to everything.

In a mechanical and depressed way she did as Manton had ordered. At half past nine she asked Count Delbos if he would take her for a walk in the garden.

'It's so hot in here,' she said, with a final look around the crowded ballroom. 'I would like some air.'

The count brought her coat, and together they walked into the gardens. The moon was high and the sky ablaze with stars. Fleur looked gloomily at these stars, her mind full of memories of Blake Carew and the hour they had spent together in this very spot.

Tonight she wore pale sea-green, a delicate foamy frock of transparent net floating to the ground, and a cape of pale green curling ostrich feather. The count was enraptured by her appearance, and told her so.

'You are more than charming, Princess. You are as beautiful as a classic picture—pure Greek, I may say. When I was in Athens . . .'

He never finished that sentence, galvanised into silence by the appearance of three men who came quickly towards them from a group of palm trees. The men took no notice of him. With rapid movements they seized Fleur. Her wrists were bound behind her. Her eyes bandaged. She struggled and screamed, as she had been directed to. A moment later she felt herself being carried rapidly across the garden. The men were doing their work well, she thought. Manton would be pleased. It was all going according to plan. In the distance she could hear the unsuspecting count raising an alarm.

She could not see, but realised that she was on the back seat of a car which started at once and roared up the hill away from the town, its exhaust crackling in the still night air. As they lurched round a series of sharp curves which she knew to be the *Moyenne Corniche*, Fleur waited for somebody to unbind her hands and eyes, but the car went on with ever-gathering speed and nobody touched her. At the end of ten minutes she began to feel angry. Manton's men were fools to carry this thing so far. She struggled and tried to call out, her heart beating fast with annoyance. Why didn't they unbind her hands? Her annoyance changed to real fear when the car pulled up with a jerk and, instead of release, she felt herself being lifted out, carried some distance, and then placed in what she guessed to be a boat. She could feel the lurch of it and hear the lap-lap of water.

What was happening? she asked herself. Why were they not at the château? She could feel the boat rocking and feel the fresh breeze coming off the sea. The *sea*! But Manton had not arranged for her to be taken out to sea.

There came the steady throb of an auxiliary engine. Fleur heard a few muffled shouts, the boat stopped. She heard the sound of footsteps on a wooden deck, and was carried up a flight of steps. Now at last she was set on her feet. Her wrists were untied and the bandage removed from her eyes.

For some moments she remained swaying unsteadily, her eyes dazzled by strong electric lights. Then as her eyes focused, she clutched feverishly at the arm of a chair beside her. This was *fantastic*! She was in the cabin of a ship and a man stood in front of her. A man who looked at her with hard, scornful eyes.

'Good evening, Miss Lorraine,' he said.

Fleur put a hand to her head and stared at him incredulously.

'Blake!'

He lit a cigarette and threw the match out of the open porthole.

'Sorry if my men were rough with you,' he said evenly. 'They aren't used to film-stunts.

64

They are my sailors.'

'Your sailors!' she repeated dully.

'Yes, Manton's men were too late,' Blake explained. 'As you may have gathered, you are on my yacht. I thought you might as well stay here instead of going back to London. I was not keen on being brought personally into your reported version of the kidnapping as a rejected suitor. I preferred to be the kidnapper-in-chief, myself. It is less humiliating.'

She continued to stare at him in amazement. She could not recognise the quiet, charming lover of the garden in this man who spoke to her with open contempt.

'I just don't understand,' she said stupidly.

'It's easy. I thought a fake kidnapping a little tame. I imagined you'd prefer a taste of the real thing.'

'But how did you find out?'

He smiled. But it was not the gay, boyish smile of the Blake she had known. His eyes were coldly sardonic. His hands when they gripped hers were like a steel vice. She felt suddenly afraid and resentful of this attitude.

'Never mind how I found out,' he said. 'I just—*did*.'

'You must be mad!'

He shrugged his shoulders.

'Perhaps. You may have heard of Mediterranean madness. Call it that, if you like.'

Fleur shrugged her shoulders. She was still

in a state of dazed surprise. But now she was also frightened. Blake was so *different.* He had altered out of all recognition. And she could see that he held her in utter contempt that broke her heart. Underneath her feet she felt a sudden gentle vibration. Somewhere on deck a bell clanged softly. Then she heard the dull throb of an engine; Blake Carew's yacht was already putting out to sea.

She stared blindly out of the porthole at the night. She felt helpless and hopeless. The throbbing of the engine echoed in her brain. She was in this man's power, a man who seemed to hate her now as deeply as she still loved him. 'Mediterranean madness' he called it. But she called it 'revenge', and she was afraid.

Blake Carew made a gesture of the hand towards a sofa which was under the porthole.

'Do sit down, please. You must be tired after your journey,' he said, in a voice of cold sarcasm.

She moved like one in a dream towards that sofa. She sat down because she felt weak and trembling at the knees. She looked dazedly round the cabin, not at all comforted by its luxury or elegance, although in normal circumstances this little saloon of a millionaire's yacht would have thrilled and pleased her. No money had been spared to make it attractive or comfortable. It was a poem in white and sealing-wax red. Red carpet, white leather chairs, white leather sofa piled with red and white cushions. Portholes framed in red linen curtains which had a white futuristic design. The cabin was flood-lit, and full of flowers, red and white carnations with fresh green fern, obviously bought in Monte Carlo that morning. The walls and ceilings were hand-painted exquisitely with nymph-like figures, floating against a blue sky. There were books and magazines in plenty. Cigarettes, cigars, boxes of sweets, a cabinet full of drinks and cut-glass tumblers. Nothing missing, Fleur noted, to make life on Blake's yacht pleasurable.

Leaning back against the cushions, trying to get her equilibrium, she watched him choose a cigar, punch it, then light it slowly and begin to smoke it without taking the slightest notice of her. Then he brought her a box of cigarettes.

'My apologies, Miss Lorraine. Please smoke.'

She took the cigarette, but said angrily:

'Do stop calling me that.'

'Do you prefer me to continue with the farce, your royal highness? Could you by any chance produce a real live king right now, for a father?'

'And stop being sarcastic.'

He laughed, and seated himself in an armchair opposite her. She noticed that he wore a white linen yachting suit with the Royal Yacht Club crest embroidered on one pocket.

He looked young and handsome in it, but in this moment she positively resented his attractiveness. She could not get away from the scorn in his eyes, his voice. It made her writhe.

'Look here, Blake,' she said, her voice, her manner a bit steadier now. 'You've got this all wrong. I don't know how you found out about me, but I swear to you that I had intended telling you the truth today, myself. I never for a moment enjoyed deceiving you.'

'I can't believe that. You enjoyed it hugely.'

'No. I did not. I loathed keeping the truth from you but I was not allowed by my directors to tell anybody about the publicity stunt . . . not even you.'

He examined the ash on his cigar, then looked at her through narrowed eyes.

'I refuse to believe that. You wanted publicity. The fact that you might hurt me in the process was incidental.'

'I swear I never wanted to hurt you.'

'It's really very humorous,' he continued, ignoring her words, 'that the first woman to whom I offered my whole heart should prove to be a fake.'

Fleur made a gesture of despair. She could see how hard it was going to be to convince him of her sincerity.

'Blake, once again, I ask you to believe me,' she said. 'I know I was a fake—that's agreed. But I didn't mean to hurt you. I tried to keep you away from me in the beginning. You know that . . .'

'In order to make me all the more keen. Hardly original, was it?'

'No,' she cried, her pain turning to bitter resentment against his attitude. 'No, that is not true. I acted a part because I was forced to.'

'Then why didn't you tell me the truth when I held you in my arms that night? You could have trusted me to keep your absurd secret.'

She winced.

'I was nervy, confused. I never dreamed you cared for me so deeply. The next morning, when I tried to see you—to tell you—I was told that you had gone.'

'It sounds plausible, my dear. But you've been delightfully plausible all along. That was a grand story about your past life—the death of your royal parents in Yugoslavia, and your education in dear England.' He laughed. 'And I fell for it, all of it. I was fool enough to lap it up and bow before your royal birth and breeding.'

Her face grew scarlet, then deadly pale.

'Must you be so bitter?'

'You have made me bitter. I looked upon you as a sweet and lovely woman, worthy of respect. Nothing is left but the loveliness—just the lovely husk.'

He put his cigar down on an ash-tray and with a swift movement seated himself beside her and caught her wrists, swinging her against

69

his body. She felt his lips on hers, crushing them in a wild kiss. It made her sick with shame and misery. But gradually under that kiss her feelings grew more wrathful, more resentful, than penitent. She regretted deceiving Blake, but he was making the most of it. He was a cad to treat her in this way. She struggled with him, tears of sheer anger magnifying her eyes, glittering on their thick lashes.

'Let me go, Blake,' she said furiously. 'You're acting like a fool.'

But Blake Carew had lost his head. Anger and desire were flaming in him. His passion for this girl swept him like an avalanche. Once again he kissed the red curve of her mouth, the cool, pale satin of her throat. He hated and wanted her. He despised and adored her. To him she was so essentially a desirable creature no matter what she had done. Deep in his heart was the desire to punish her for making a fool of him, but his passion for her was uppermost in this hour.

Before she had come into his life he had been a cynic about women and love. He had taken kisses as carelessly as he drank champagne. He had always made sure that he would not suffer one heartache. Fleur, 'The Princess', had swept all that aside. His vision had been clouded by her beauty. He had been blinded by her apparent goodness and sweet dignity.

At length he let her go and returned to sanity.

'Don't cry, my dear,' he said, looking down at her. She had hidden her face in the cushions. 'To hell with the past and the future. From now on, I intend to live for the present and you can make it amusing for me.'

In a muffled voice she said:

'You're cruel, Blake. Utterly cruel.'

'*You* speak of cruelty, when you won your way into my heart, only to smash my ideals— make a damned idiot out of me.'

'You can't forgive me for being an actress? I was in need of money and success.'

'Your poverty would have meant nothing to me and I don't blame you for being an actress. It's an honest profession—as a rule—but I worshipped you because I thought you a simple and sincere person. I realise now that you never intended to marry me. You can't marry two men at the same time without committing bigamy, can you?'

Raising her head, she looked at him incredulously.

'What are you talking about?'

He smiled bitterly.

'I happened to overhear Mark Manton saying you were to marry him on your return to London.'

For a moment Fleur felt incapable of replying. The position was becoming untenable. What had Mark been saying about

71

her? What other lies had Blake heard which had blackened her in his sight? When she spoke, her voice was a whisper.

'That's another lie. Mark means nothing to me. I have never had the slightest intention of marrying him. If you believe everything against me—why bother to keep me? Please order your crew to take me back to the shore.'

Blake was still holding her hands. She tried vainly to release them, beginning to feel very tired. She ceased struggling, and her head suddenly dropped against his shoulder. She heard his voice as from a great distance.

'It would be foolish of me to send you back, my dear Fleur,' he was saying. 'I need you here. I told you this is no play-acting. It is *fact*. You are going to stay on my yacht until I grow tired of the game.'

Her eyes opened, beseeching him.

'Blake, *please!*'

'Why worry? It's a fine idea. We can have a lot of fun. We were excellent companions on shore—why not at sea?'

She stared at him dumbly, wondering what he meant to do—what he meant by saying he intended to keep her on the yacht until he grew tired of the game. A dozen different conjectures leaped to her mind, and left her shaken. They were interrupted by a knock on the door.

Blake took his cigar up from the ash-tray again.

'Come in,' he said curtly.

The door opened. A heavily built man in sailor's uniform, a blue-and-white cap at a rakish angle on his curly head, stood staring curiously at her. Fleur looked back at him. She wondered whether this man, or any other member of the crew, would listen to her if she appealed to him to help her escape.

She met the gaze of two burning dark eyes. Strange, glittering eyes in a dead-white face, with high cheekbones, This sailor was an extraordinary-looking man and definitely foreign, she told herself. There was something about him which made her flesh creep. When he looked at her his eyes seemed to bore through her. It was not a pleasant look.

'Excuse please, sir,' he said in a deep, ringing voice.

'What is it, Renzo?' Blake asked.

'Mr. Benson is in dinner saloon, sir. He would like to see you for a moment.'

'Right, tell him I'll come.'

Blake turned back to Fleur, his face thoughtful.

'You look scared,' he said. 'Have you seen a ghost?'

'It's that sailor; he has such peculiar eyes.'

Blake threw back his head and laughed.

'I'm not surprised. He probably hates you. He spent some years in Russia. He has a healthy dislike of *l'aristocratie.* No doubt some Tartar princess gave him a touch of the *knout.'*

Fleur shuddered.

'It's horrible,' she said. '*He* hates me. You hate me. The whole atmosphere is—sinister. I'm frightened, Blake. And I've had enough, I tell you. You must let me go.'

He came back to the sofa and caught her in his arms again.

'You needn't be afraid of Renzo—or of anybody. You will be completely spoiled here—by me. Your voyage will consist of peace, sunshine, moonlight, love and kisses. You can't say you haven't got the correct setting for a romance. Don't you like my saloon? And if you follow me you shall see your private suite.'

She was still weak and dazed as he took her arm and led her to the cabin-de-luxe which he said was to be hers. She saw the luxury of the little white-and-gold room; amber silk curtains drawn across the portholes, a soft thick carpet, a table with a Lalique bowl of yellow roses, roses everywhere. Bedstead with exquisite embroidered linen, and gold satin spread. Shaded lamps and electric fire. The luxury of it seemed to augment her misery.

'I loathe it—loathe the whole yacht. I prefer to be back in my hotel.'

He held her closer to his body, his face against hers, his fingers threading through her hair.

'But you are going to stay here, Fleur. You are mine. You can pretend this is a honeymoon cruise. You're a good actress, so it shouldn't be difficult. Just act your new role, darling, as well as you acted the old one, only this time you must imagine yourself as my wife instead of a lonely princess . . . I'm going to leave you now. You'll find clothes in that cupboard. I shan't be long. Dress for our celebration, darling; all the "props" you need are here.'

She shrank back in his arms.

'You are mad, Blake—absolutely crazy.'

'You have yourself to blame. Nobody else in the world!'

He picked her right up in his arms and carried her to the bed. Her head fell back against the pillows. He bent down and pressed a long obliterating kiss on her lips.

'In half an hour,' he said thickly. 'Drinks, supper on the deck—and music. Then we'll share the wonders of a Mediterranean night.'

When he had gone, Fleur lay with her hands pressed to her breast, her cheeks flaming, her heart beating with sickening jerks. She could hear the throb of the engines increasing in intensity. The yacht was beginning to sway slightly. They must be well out to sea. She gave a little sob of a laugh, telling herself it was a good thing she could boast of being a splendid sailor.

If only Blake would listen to reason and try to understand, the position would be bearable. But she felt it was hopeless. It was futile to argue with him in his present mood. He was the very antithesis of the man she had known in Monte Carlo. Under his first kiss she had learned all the real ecstasy of love; the one intense love which had ever entered her life. His attitude tonight hurt and humiliated her. Indeed, it was intolerable anguish, an anguish made worse by the fact that she still loved him.

Slowly she rose from the bed and drew back the curtains from one of the portholes. There was a light shining on deck. Then the sea— calm, rippling sea, flooded with moonlight. Overhead the sky was a blanket of twinkling stars. It was a glorious tranquil night.

As she stood there, Fleur thought of her home in Streatham Hill, and of her mother and sister. They seemed a million miles away, in another world. What would they say, poor dears, when they did not hear from her? What would Mark and the rest of them at the studios do? There would be a genuine police hunt for her now. No publicity stunt.

She drew back from the porthole and stared bleakly around the fascinating cabin. Through a half-open door she could see a perfect little bathroom—sea-green with a silver bath. She remembered Blake's words: *'You must imagine yourself my wife instead of a lonely princess.'* A threat lay behind that speech—a threat of further humiliation at his hands.

'What shall I do?' she asked herself. 'What shall I do? I loved you, Blake. I love you now.

If only you knew!'

Suddenly she stood back and raised her head. She could hear a faint knock on the porthole through which she had just been looking. Her heart missed a beat. Opening the glass, she looked out and felt a new spasm of fear. It was the sailor Renzo.

'What do you want?' she called.

'To speak with you, Princess,' he replied in a whisper.

'What have you to say to me?'

'I want to help you, Highness. Tell me if there is any service I can render. I know that you are being held a prisoner. When I saw you, you seemed to ask for my help. I have come to offer it.'

There was a tense silence. The night breeze fanned the curtains across the man's face. Fleur held them back and tried to think clearly. Why did this sinister fellow—this refugee from Russia—pity her and offer his help? It seemed strange and unreal. Blake had said that Renzo hated her. Or had Blake only said that to frighten her?

'Do you really want to help me?' she asked in a low tone.

'Yes, Princess. Tell me what to do.'

'Can you get me off this boat?'

'Maybe. We stop now. Anchor for the night.'

'Then,' she said, 'take me back to shore now—at once.'

'It would be dangerous.'

'But you can manage it—somehow. You will be well paid. I promise you a large sum of money.'

The sailor ran a hand across his untidy black hair. Then he nodded. A queer, pleased look came into his eyes. Looking down both ends of the deck, he put a finger to his lips.

'I hear officer of the watch,' he said quickly. 'No, I am wrong. There is nobody there. Mr. Carew is with captain in the dining-saloon. They should be busy for another ten minutes. Engines stopping now.'

'You mean I can come out now?' Fleur asked breathlessly.

He nodded.

'When you leave cabin, turn to the left and up gangway. I will meet you there.'

'I understand.'

She felt suddenly wild with excitement.

Shutting the porthole, she ran across the floor of the cabin. Her nerves were tingling. Her mind elated with relief. She had only one ambition now—to get out of this place right away front the yacht before Blake could stop her.

Throwing her coat across her shoulders, she turned the handle of the door. It opened noiselessly to her touch. There was silence outside, save for the slight rocking of the anchored yacht. A moment later she was on the starlit deck.

The man was waiting for her. He looked at

her intently. In the moonlight her face had an almost unearthly beauty. But he saw no beauty in it. His heart was dark with hatred. His vision warped and distorted.

'You ready, Princess?' he asked.

'Yes.' (She did not bother to disillusion him as to her real identity.)

'Then come, quickly.'

The deck was deserted to starboard. There was nobody to see the dinghy being lowered to the water, nor watch it pulling away from the side of the yacht.

The small boat rocked on the rippling tide. Sitting in the stern, Fleur looked back and saw the lights from the portholes of the yacht gleaming like rosy circles in the velvet night. Her heart beat fast. For once in his life Blake was not to get his own way, she thought triumphantly.

At the same time she felt utterly wretched. She had loved him, and never again would she see that handsome face, not know the blinding passion of his kisses. It was over. She had said good-bye to Blake Carew and all he stood for. They would never meet again.

Her eyes began to fill with tears. Turning her gaze from the yacht, she looked towards the coast. Her wrist-watch told her that it was eleven o'clock. Monte Carlo was just waking up. Lights twinkled and sparkled like fireflies all along the shore.

Suddenly she became aware that the sailor

was staring at her. Staring at her in a sinister, penetrating way which brought her abruptly to her senses and dispelled any other thoughts.

'Well,' she said nervously, 'when should we get to the shore?'

'*Never!*'

The word was like the snap of a bullet across the still night air. Fleur's heart jerked madly. A nauseating sensation of fear seized her. Renzo was now looking at her with eyes which were frankly hostile. He was no longer rowing. The wet, dripping oars lay against the side of the boat. He was leaning towards her, his hands gripping his knees.

'What are you talking about?' she asked hoarsely. 'Why do you stare at me?'

'You would like to command me,' he said slowly. 'But you cannot. I am not your dog— your servant. I am my own master now. Do not wish take you to the land.'

Fleur put a hand to her throat where a frightened pulse was beating.

'What are you going to do, then?'

'To kill you! One more royalty—pah!' He spat into the water.

'You're mistaken, Renzo,' she said. She licked her dry lips. 'I am no princess. I swear it ... In actual fact I am just an ordinary English lady.'

'Ah, I know all about you,' he broke in. 'I have read about you since you came to Monte Carlo. I read about you in the papers. The

80

aristocratic wealthy Princess Fleur! Bah! I hate the cursed blood which runs in your veins.'

She shrank back in her seat. There was something devilish in this creature's bearded face. He was a madman. She realised that too late. She had escaped from Blake only to pitch herself headlong into the hands of a maniac.

He began to pour out a torrent of wild, abusive words. She understood what he was trying to tell her. He spoke of his years in Siberia, and of the punishment he had suffered. He was Italian, but he had been a servant in the employ of a Tartar princess. She had stood by, in her furs and diamonds, while the *knout* had torn into his back.

'I can show you scars,' he snarled. 'I have never forgotten. Always I have waited for my revenge. Now I shall take it . . .'

Fleur saw him lunge towards her. She sprang up, a cry of stark terror on her lips. The boat gave a violent lurch. For a split second it seemed to balance in mid-air. Then it was over. A cold blanket of water rushed towards her. She struggled madly. It was too late. She was going down. The water was in her mouth and lungs, stifling her cries. She was being pulled under as if by an unseen hand. She was drowning.

CHAPTER SIX

Fleur came to the surface, gasping and choking. Through half-blinded eyes she could see that the mad sailor was close beside her, moving his arms and legs in the water. He was trying to reach her.

'Death to princess—death!' he was shouting in a wild choked voice.

With a superhuman effort she began to strike out in the opposite direction. She was a good strong swimmer, but her heavy coat and dress clung to her and weighed her down, and she was already weak with shock and fright. She sent up a desperate cry.

'Help!'

Renzo gave a spluttering laugh. She could see that he was drawing nearer to her. Tearing at the hook of her fur coat, she managed to drop it from her shoulders. Her flimsy dress did little to impede her progress, and now she could make headway, well on top of the water.

A moment later she heard a voice across the water. *Blake's voice.*

'Where are you? Call again.'

'Here,' she shouted. '*I'm here, here . . . here! . . .*'

She knew then that he had heard. He was coming to her. Renzo knew it too, and with a choking cry of rage tried to catch up with her.

The sailor was too late. A motor-boat cut swiftly through the sea, its hull making great curves of creamy foam. Blake and another man were in the boat, which was at full throttle. Blake himself crouched at the wheel, his face white, his eyes bright with fear. He knew what had happened. When he discovered that Fleur had gone he had guessed Renzo had gone with her. He had always been a little afraid of the crazy refugee whom he had taken only out of kindness aboard the yacht.

Fleur knew no more until, opening her eyes, she found that she was lying on the bed in her cabin, once more on the yacht. She was flat on her back. Blake and one of his officers were bending over her. They had been applying artificial respiration.

'I'm all right,' she whispered. 'Thank God!'

She heard Blake's voice.

'Yes, you're fine. She'll be all right now, Benson. You can go.'

'Yes, sir. Shall I send up some coffee?'

'Yes, and cognac.'

'Very good, sir.'

Once again Fleur opened her heavy eyelids. She saw Blake's face, stern and inscrutable. He looked down at her.

'You nearly died that time.'

'It was horrible—horrible. He's a *maniac*.'

Blake nodded.

'I knew he was queer, but I had no idea he was dangerous.'

'Where is he?'

'In irons. We'll put him off at our next stop. He's Italian, like the rest of the hands. They're a damned nuisance, but all I could get.'

Fleur drew a broken sigh and put a hand to her head. She was still in her soaking dress, a torn, limp rag of a once-lovely gown. Water trickled from it, making a pool on the bedspread. Her chestnut hair was plastered to her head. She drew her hands over her face and shuddered.

'I can get up now,' she said. 'I feel better.'

Bending down, Blake lifted her in his arms. She began to protest, but felt too weak. When she was on her feet, he took a heavy silk dressing-gown from the cupboard and handed it to her.

'Put that on and get back to bed and keep warm.' His voice was rough. He refused to meet her beseeching gaze. 'I'll hurry up with that coffee.'

Fleur felt incapable of further argument. Her experience with Renzo seemed to have drained her last vestige of resistance. After Blake shut the door behind him, she sat for a moment on the edge of the bed, uncontrolled tears running down her cheeks. It was, she realised, growing late now. Dawn would soon be breaking. She would be forced to stay in the yacht, at least until morning. She had better make the best of it. It was Hobson's choice.

Struggling feebly with her clothes, she

84

managed to get them off, and putting on the dressing-gown, she climbed into bed. She was grateful for the hot-water bottles which she found there. In spite of the warmth of the cabin her whole body was chilled and shivering.

When Blake returned, carrying a tray of coffee and brandy, she was just beginning to feel warmer and a little less shattered. There was some colour in her cheeks. A colour which deepened to scarlet as Blake approached the bed.

He looked down at her. She had rubbed her wet hair with a rough towel and it was curling all over her head. It made her look extraordinarily young and rather pathetic. There was no make-up on the pale young face.

'Drink this,' he said, placing the tray within her reach.

'No . . .' she began.

'Don't be a fool. Drink it.'

Shrugging her shoulders, she picked up a cup and sipped the steaming coffee. She felt really grateful for it. The cognac in it revived her still more. When the cup was empty, Blake refilled it with brandy.

'I don't want any more,' she told him.

'Of course you do,' he said, gripping her wrists. 'It'll make you less scared of me—more like the girl I knew in Monte Carlo.'

'You were different then,' she flashed back. 'This is only your vile wish to punish me.'

'It was vile of you to trick me, if we are using that ugly word.'

Her eyes pleaded with him.

'Blake, don't be so hard—you are quite mad with longing to be revenged on me. It is making you lose your sense of proportion.'

He laughed, leaned down and kissed her damp, curly hair and her cool, pale throat.

'Don't worry about tonight,' he said. 'You can sleep in peace. Tomorrow, we'll make up for lost time.'

For a long time she lay with her head buried in the pillows, her body shaken with sobs. When, at last, she opened her eyes it was to find him gone.

During those next difficult hours she tried to forget that they had ever loved each other. She did not want to remember that the restless aching of her heart had been lulled in the warmth and tenderness of his embrace. The present position was a travesty of those other days. How she regretted her pose of Princess! But it had seemed innocent enough. If only Blake had been a comparatively poor man it would have been less complicated. Obviously, he must think that she had hoped to get money from him.

That night she slept badly. Her nerves were on fire; her dreams were of a mad sailor who kept staring at her with glittering eyes. When he leaped towards her she awoke to find herself stifling a scream and bathed in perspiration.

She rose soon after the dawn broke through the night. Her head ached badly. Rest was out of the question. Searching in the cupboard, she found a blue soft wool jumper, with a polo collar and some grey flannel slacks. There were a pair of gay Spanish *espadrilles* which fitted her small bare feet. She put these things on, combed her hair, put a touch of make-up on her haggard young face, and, feeling more herself, walked out of the cabin.

On deck she stood a moment by the rails. She found the morning fresh and radiant. During the night the yacht had put out to sea again. Now land was barely visible, the coast no more than a thin grey line. Around her the sea glittered like blown glass. The sky was blue and unclouded. A fresh breeze brought some colour to Fleur's cheeks as she stood there, arms folded, staring at the horizon. A gull winged overhead, uttering a raucous screech before it dipped down into the translucent water.

The beauty of the scene spread before Fleur's eyes—the trim white yacht swaying gently on the shimmering peacock-blue of the sea—stimulated her. For a fleeting moment she toyed with the thought of jumping overboard into the calm waters and swimming to shore, but immediately abandoned the idea. She might be a strong swimmer, but five miles in any sea would be suicide. And she had had enough drowning last night.

Her only hope, she decided, was to appeal to another member of the crew. There was certainly one officer on board. Benson, the man who had helped Blake give her artificial respiration last night. He was an Englishman. It was possible that he might believe her story and help her.

When, some minutes later, she looked round, she saw Mr. Benson stepping down from the bridge. She walked towards him, her cheeks flaming with colour.

'Good morning, Mr. Benson,' she said.

The officer stopped to look at her. He was a slim, fair-haired young man with light-blue eyes. For five years he had been in Blake's service, during which time his master had become his god. It was Blake who had saved his family from financial ruin. Blake who had put him in charge of this yacht at a wildly generous salary. Fleur found herself appealing to the wrong man.

'I'm afraid I can't stay and talk,' he said, when she started her appeal. 'Mr. Carew does not care for the crew to associate with his guests.'

Touching his cap, he walked firmly away. She looked after him with despair.

The silent gloom which had become instilled in her lasted for the rest of the morning. At nine o'clock the yacht raised anchor and moved further out to sea. By now,

Fleur told herself, the papers would have got on to her disappearance, but nobody would associate it with Blake. Nobody, except perhaps Mark, who might notice Blake's sudden departure from Monte Carlo. But if he did, what use would it be? Nobody would find the yacht, and perhaps, when it was disclosed that she was an actress seeking publicity, the authorities would not even bother to look for her.

The rest of the day was a nightmare. She was forced to eat her meals with Blake, and spend the afternoon sitting with him on the sunbaked deck. He was scrupulously attentive, but always behind his immaculate courtesy she detected contempt. His voice held a mocking note. Although he neither touched nor attempted to kiss her, she was conscious that passion lay dormant within him. It smouldered in his grey eyes, ready to leap up into flame for her.

As the day turned to night her fears increased. Before dinner she stood in the starlight wondering how best to deal with the disaster which was coming upon her in a headlong crash. If Blake carried this thing to extremes tonight, he would, she knew, hate himself afterwards—and hate her even more. Their love-dream of the past would be trampled on and irrevocably ruined.

At seven o'clock, when Blake had gone to his cabin to change his clothes, Fleur, in a state of acute nerves, began to wander round the decks. Eventually she found herself in a part of the ship which she did not know, but imagined to be the crew's quarters. Hesitating outside the door of the cabin, she heard the sound of men's voices. They were speaking Italian. One man, talking in a low, decisive voice, held her attention. She recognised his soft Ligurian accent and thanked heaven she was fluent in this language as well as French.

'Tonight,' he was saying, 'at midnight. Is it agreed?'

There was a murmur of assent, followed by the voice of another man.

'You think we can manage it?'

'Of course we can. *Santa Maria!* There's not a man on board against us except the Maestro and Signor Benson.'

'What will you do with them?'

'Put them in the irons which Renzo is wearing. Then we need only take the boat and make for Ventimiglia.'

Fleur crouched against the door, her brain working swiftly. She could not fail to understand It was mutiny. Blake's Italian crew were traitors.

'We can settle the men,' said another voice. 'What about the girl?'

'Let her come with us,' replied the man who was obviously the leader. 'She should be good company!'

A ripple of laughter followed his words.

90

'Agreed!'

'Midnight, then,' repeated the leader. 'First to Benson's cabin. We'll fix him. Then to the girl's. The Maestro will be there. We'll get him cold.'

Fleur turned and ran along the deck, afraid that she might be seen by one of the men. It was an amazing conversation which she had overheard. She now had Blake in the hollow of her hand. If the crew mutinied, he would be powerless. The sailors apparently felt quite friendly towards her. They were Italians and could not resist a pretty face. She could go with them to Ventimiglia and then work her way back through Menton to Monte Carlo.

As soon as she crossed the French frontier she would inform the authorities, and they would send out to rescue Blake and Benson. There could be no danger for the Englishmen, but at the same time the thought of abandoning them troubled her conscience. She wondered what had upset the crew. Probably some petty grievance. Blake had told her they were an untrustworthy lot.

What should she do? This was a heaven-sent opportunity for escape from Blake. She had only to speak to the sailors and they would take her. On the other hand, if she warned Blake and Benson they might subdue the crew and keep her on board. She must either warn Blake and remain in his hands, or keep silent and return to land.

When she entered her cabin she looked pensive and agitated. Blake was already there, fixing a red carnation in the buttonhole of his dinner-jacket.

'I was waiting for you,' he said. 'Where have you been?'

'On deck. I wanted some air.'

'And I want a kiss,' he laughed, moving towards her.

Putting her hands on his shoulders, Fleur tried to push him away.

'Let me alone, Blake. You make me tired.'

'How you have changed, Princess!'

She twisted round, her dark eyes blazing.

'Don't call me that!'

If he had noticed the warning note in her voice he might have hesitated before mocking her again, but he continued in the same almost arrogant fashion.

'*Pour un peu d'amour, un peu d'amour,*' he sang in French, pressing his face against hers, '*Jé donnerai bien mes nuits, mes jours.*'

'You fool,' she began. 'I think . . .'

He stopped the rest of her sentence, closing her lips with a long kiss.

'Princess, Flower of all women,' he murmured. 'Women like you shouldn't think. They should just be content to look beautiful.'

She clenched her hands. Her eyes gleamed at him with passionate resentment. He gave her little choice. She could not trust him. She felt convinced that if she warned him about the trouble he would get the men under control and prevent it. He had a masterful personality. The Italians would be like putty in his hands. He would make them change their minds, and she would find herself in the same position. It would begin all over again. She would be humiliated, insulted by his passion, knowing how little he loved or respected her.

'I despise you,' she said. 'I never thought any man could be such a cad.'

'Sorry, my dear. I told you I had become ruthless.'

'And you are making me the same,' she said, with hot tears in her eyes. 'I warn you, Blake. You'll drive me too far.'

'What will you do?'

'I don't know—yet.'

'Shall I tell you?' he whispered against her ear. 'For a little while you'll be angry, furious, proud. You'll enjoy pretending to be all these things. You'll dramatise yourself, but in the end you'll become normal—just yourself. You'll be pleased with your adventures on the yacht. You'll be able to entertain your future admirers for weeks with your reminiscenses.'

'I'll never forgive you for that,' she said, breathing fast. 'Never.'

'Yet I find it so easy to forgive anything when you are in my arms,' he mocked. 'Your hair is like the satin of chestnuts with the sun on them. Your lips are scarlet curves of sheer delight. Tonight they will be absolutely mine.'

She was silent. In spite of her efforts to appear calmly disdainful of his passion, she was trembling from head to foot. She had reached her decision. His last words had forced the issue. She knew now what she intended to do. She was finished with Blake. She would leave the yacht with the Italians.

'There will be no "tonight", Blake,' she told him.

'Won't there?' he said, with a self-confident smile. 'And why not?'

For a moment he looked at her thoughtfully. He had tried to persuade himself that her attraction for him was now purely physical, but had to admit it was not altogether so. He was unhappy, tormented. He found only bitter pleasure in the treatment he was meting out to her. He wanted to despise her and be indifferent to her feelings. He could not. It only ended up by him despising himself. When he thought of her trembling in his arms he felt a despicable brute, yet he could not draw back.

He tried to tell himself that Fleur Lorraine was merely a good actress, that she had never cared for him and that she deserved punishment. He must carry on—make her pay. Only in the kisses which he would extract from her would he find release from his own aching heart.

When he turned from her, his voice was unnaturally gay. He said:

'What you need, my dear girl, is a drink. You're getting introspective and morbid. Change your clothes while I mix you a cocktail. It shall be a special mixture for you and we will christen it *"Ce soir ou jamais".*'

'Tonight or never!' Her blood beat in her brain as she watched him move slowly, smilingly, out of her cabin.

CHAPTER SEVEN

That night Blake Carew appeared to all intents and purposes to be in the highest of sports. At dinner he enjoyed his food, toasted Fleur in charnpagne, and kept up an amusing commentary to which she made no effort to respond.

She sat silent, listening, and watching him. She felt acutely conscious of the sinister atmosphere which permeated the boat. It was easy to read the thoughts on the faces of the sailors. Even the steward who served their meal looked pale, almost scared, and could not conceal his anxiety.

After dinner they went out on deck, where Blake sat beside Fleur facing the moon-silvered sea. For some time he amused himself by playing dance-records on a portable gramophone. Holding her hands in his, he told her that she looked exquisite in the soft starlight, that this night was the correct setting for her beauty.

Fleur let him do and say what he wished. She was almost ashamed of her feminine weakness and vanity because she had consented to put on one of the dresses in her wardrobe. A long tight skirt of black cloth, a delicate chiffon evening blouse, a short black dinner coat with white flowers pinned to the lapel. A white flower in her hair.

He was perplexed by her. She seemed so quiet and meek—so accessible and acquiescent that it baffled him. He preferred her to fight, to protest against him. Tonight she was mute and motionless. It was like making love to a beautiful statue, and he grew weary of it.

As the hour arranged by the crew for action drew nearer, Fleur became restive. The strain of anticipation began to tell on her. It was almost midnight when Blake noticed how white she looked. Her eyes were abnormally large and bright. At once he felt concern.

'Are you feeling ill?' he asked.

She shook her head.

'No. Why do you ask?'

He bent to touch her hair with his lips.

'You look—not yourself. But it's late. Come down to the cabin.'

Fleur shivered. As she turned to walk beside him along the deck she felt like a traitor. But it was his own fault. He had shown her no mercy.

There was no reason why she should show him any or spoil her own chance of winning this game.

Blake's cabin was next to her own. At his door he stopped.

'There is champagne waiting on the ice for us. Will you join me?'

Fleur nodded.

'Yes! I want my handkerchief. I'll be back in a minute.'

She trembled as she switched on the light in her cabin. Her nerves were on edge. There seemed to be shadows lurking in every corner, shadows of men ready to spring. Once again she had to check her natural instinct, which was to warn Blake. Her lips were already forming his name when she heard sounds which drained the blood from her face.

Then came the sound of Blake's voice raised in protest. A few staccato Italian words. The noise of overturned furniture. The sickening crunch of a blow and the dull thud of a body falling on the floor. A low drawn-out moan.

Fleur's heart seemed to stop beating. Staggering back, she leaned against the lintel of the door. This was something for which she had not bargained. The men had attacked Blake personally. She cursed herself for a fool. It was what she might have expected from a lot of cowardly Italians. She experienced a sickening revulsion of feeling and remorse.

She was aghast because they might have killed him, and she could have warned him. If he were dead, she would be responsible.

A moment later the feeling of self-preservation conquered all others. If it was too late to save Blake, she could at least try to save herself. Only by getting to the shore and appealing for assistance could she hope to help *him*.

Moving quietly from her cabin, she listened at the next door. There was a low murmur of conversation. Then she recognised the voice of the sailor whom she had heard making plans earlier in the day.

'That's fixed him,' the man was saying. 'He won't come round for the best part of an hour. The other boys have got Signor Benson. We'll leave them both in the hold.'

A little of the colour returned to Fleur's face. So Blake was unconscious, but not badly hurt.

'What about the girl?' said another voice.

'We'll get her later. Leave her until we're ready.'

'Very good. What about a drink?'

Once again the leader spoke.

'Leave the drink alone. We've got to get off this yacht—and get off quickly. There's hell's own storm blowing up. We must move before it breaks.'

Fleur stood staring round her. If there were a storm on the way it would mean certain death for Blake and Benson. The yacht would probably get out of hand and be swept toward the jagged coast. There was only one thing to be done. She must hide, let the Italians get off without her, and then get to Blake and set him free.

She ran up on deck and saw that the moon was hidden now behind a heavy bank of cloud. Already the *mistral* was troubling the water. The men were right. The sky was overcast and ominous. She knew that very soon not a solitary star would show in the darkness of the skies.

For a moment, however, she was glad of the darkness. Creeping along by the rail, she came to a large coil of rope covered by a tarpaulin. In the centre of the coil there was a cavity large enough for her to get into. Stepping over the rope, she crouched down and pulled the canvas over her, leaving a space through which she could breathe and see as far as the end of the boat.

Long afterwards she was to remember the horror and suspense of the next minutes. The yacht began to sway violently against the quickly gathering swell. There was the sound of footsteps, of men tramping up and down the decks, calling her name in rough, urgent voices. And, finally, the angry tones of the leader.

'*Sapristi!* Let her go. It's starting to rain. The storm will be on us at any moment.

Andiamo!'

Fleur lay still under the stifling tarpaulin, hardly daring to breath. Not until all was quiet did she dare to lift the cover and look out. Not a man was to be seen. The yacht appeared completely deserted. The engines had stopped. There was an almost deathly silence and stillness. Then far out on the shadowy water she saw the slim shape of a boat pulling steadily away from the yacht. The crew had abandoned ship and were making for the shore.

A moment later she felt heavy raindrops blown by the wind against her face. From a distance there came a low growl of thunder. She felt suddenly afraid—afraid of the darkness and the sinister quiet of the deserted yacht.

Turning, she ran along the deck and down the steep iron stairs to the hold in the depths of the boat. A small hurricane lamp burned with a flickering light. Then she saw the two men who lay side by side on the floor. Mr. Benson lay quite still, and for a moment she thought he was dead. Then all her concentration was focused on the other figure. Blake! Blake, who lay on his back, his face a white mask of pain in the dim light.

She fell on her knees beside him.

'Blake!' she cried hoarsely. 'Oh God, what have they done to you? Speak to me, Blake, *speak . . .'*

His eyes opened slowly. He looked ghastly in the dim light of the hurricane lamp which swung shadows across his face. A thin line of blood trickled from a gash below his eye. He groaned as he looked towards her.

'Traitors—dirty traitors!' he muttered.

She drew back. So he thought her one of the men who had brought him down to the hold. The gash under his eye was still bleeding slowly and must have sapped his strength. He had found himself up against insurmountable odds. He could have had no chance, and the last blow on the temple had finished him off.

Fleur felt sick and faint. Pulling a handkerchief from her pocket, she tried to staunch the blood. Blake groaned again.

'Damn you—you greasy swine!'

She looked from Blake to Benson in despair. What could she do? How could she make them realise their danger? By now the crew would be well away. There was little doubt that the yacht was drifting. The distant rumble of thunder heralded the approaching storm. Anything might happen to them all— and at any moment. They might run aground or sink without the men knowing anything about it. She began calling Blake's name.

'Blake! Make an effort! Try to understand what I'm saying to you!'

Slowly, as she watched him, the mists began to clear away from his mind. He raised himself on an elbow, groaned and wiped away the blood from his eyes with the back of his hand.

'Hell!' he muttered. 'What's happened? Where am I?' Then, as he saw the pale face of the girl who bent over him: 'Fleur! Tell me what happened . . .'

'Thank God you can speak,' she said, choking back her sobs. 'Are you badly hurt?'

He blinked and shook his head. For a moment he covered his face with his hands. She could see that his head was hurting him.

'I'm all right. I think it's only a flesh-wound. More blood than anything. You must have been pretty scared.'

She did not answer. She could not trust herself to speak, but held a clenched hand against her lips as Blake looked up and around him.

'Mutiny!' he said, as though speaking to himself. 'I remember now. They caught me one over the head when I went into my cabin. The swine! I never dreamed they were working up to a show like this. Where are they now? What happened to you? Are you all right?'

She nodded.

'Yes. I hid till they'd gone.'

'Gone! Where?'

'To Ventimiglia. In the boat. There isn't a soul left on the yacht. The engines have stopped.'

He wiped his face with his coat sleeve. His mind was clearing every second.

'The hell they have! Then we must be drifting.'

'And there's a storm blowing up.'

He set his teeth.

'Help me to my feet, Fleur. Something must be done—and done quickly. If we could only get this head to stop bleeding, I can probably help matters. Help me along to my cabin. There's a first-aid outfit there. You can see to the wound.'

Fleur went quickly up to him.

'Lean on my shoulder,' she said. 'When I've done your head we'll try to fix up Benson.'

'Benson!' he repeated.

She pointed towards the figure which lay motionless in a dark corner of the hold.

'Yes. He looks pretty bad.'

Blake looked in the direction of his officer and cursed under his breath.

'So they got him too?'

'They got him first.'

He turned to look into her eyes.

'How do you know?' he said quickly.

A wave of colour dyed her face and throat.

'I overheard them—plotting it all.'

He stared at her incredulously.

'And you mean to say you let them do it? You didn't warn me?'

She flung back her head with a semblance of defiance.

'Why should I have done? You showed *me* no mercy.'

'I see,' he answered with a curt laugh. 'So you would have watched our throats being cut, with pleasure.'

'That's not true,' she protested. 'I never imagined they meant to do you any personal harm. If I had, I would obviously have told and warned you.'

Blake shrugged his shoulders.

'Well, as it is,' he said dryly, 'you won't gain much. We'll quite probably drift into the teeth of an almighty storm and flounder. And we'll still be together, my dear, you and I.'

She stood up, trembling and flushed, and nearly in tears again. It rose to her lips to tell him that she could refuse to help him to his cabin, that she could refuse to help him get the drifting vessel under control. He was weak and obviously ill from loss of blood. His heart might let him down at any moment. And Benson was also in a precarious condition. If she chose, she could leave them and trust to luck that the yacht would drift into shore where she could get away.

But the sight of Blake's blood-smeared face and pain-filled eyes was more than she could bear. She was essentially a woman—and she had loved him. She took his arm with a firm hand.

'Let's drop it now, Blake. We're all in a tight corner. Why not forget petty grievances and think of our lives.'

He stood swaying a little dizzily under the

touch of her hand, his fingers pressed to his eyes.

'You could have warned me, and you didn't,' he repeated. 'I don't call that "petty".'

She made a gesture of impatience.

'I'm going to see to your head now. For heaven's sake, hurry up.'

Leaning heavily on her arm, Blake had begun to walk with her across the uneven floor of the hold, when a sudden moan from Benson attracted their attention. For a moment they looked in the direction of the sound. Then the officer began to speak.

'Mr. Carew! Are you there, sir?'

Going towards him, Blake dropped to one knee and raised the man's head.

'I'm here, Benson. How do you feel?'

Benson touched the top of his head with a finger.

'Not too bad, sir. They must have cracked me a beauty. There's a lump like an egg here. But I'm all right.'

'Then we must try to get the yacht under control,' Blake said urgently. 'There's a storm brewing, and those swine have cleared off with the boat.'

'I wonder what got under their skins,' muttered Benson. 'I didn't sense trouble in the offing.'

'No more did I. But don't waste time worrying about them now.'

'No, sir. But I'd give something to meet

them again.'

'So would I,' said Blake grimly. 'Once we get back to shore we'll see about that. I'm going to my cabin to fix this head. You'd better try the radio, if you can get there. Send out an S O S.'

'Very good, sir.'

Between them, Fleur and Blake managed to raise Benson to his feet. He stood swaying, grinning sheepishly at the girl.

The two men walked on each side of Fleur. She was pale and quiet. Inwardly half-remorseful for not having warned them, yet still resentful of the hostile attitude which Blake persisted in showing her. With difficulty she helped the two men up the steep iron steps which led to the deck. As they turned the corner they were met by the full fury of the storm which had not been so noticeable down in the hold. A keen, angry gale was already blowing up, lashing the sea into great surging waves which broke over the decks of the yacht. The sky was black and starless against a heavy curtain of rain.

It was all that Fleur could do to keep her feet on the slippery wood. The yacht lurched heavily against her shoulders. Not until they reached the wireless cabin, where Benson shut himself in, was she able to make any real progress. Then she heard Blake shouting at her above the screaming wind.

'This looks pretty tricky,' he grinned.

'You're going to regret not having warned me, my dear. Looks as though you'll find a watery grave—in my arms.'

'If I'm going to drown, it won't be in your arms,' she shouted back. 'You haven't won yet.'

When they reached Blake's cabin it was to find it in complete confusion. Broken bottles and smashed ivories were on the floor. Bedclothes ripped from the bed. Curtains and cushions slashed. Drawers turned out and looted. Little of value was left. The crew appeared to have broken the place up out of the sheer desire to plunder and spoil. The saloon through which they had passed was in the same disorder and chaos. The exquisite murals had been torn from the walls.

Sitting down on his bed, Blake rested his head between his hands. He tried to laugh.

'A pretty good show,' he muttered. 'They certainly did things well while they were about it. Oh God, this ruddy head of mine is swimming. You might try to find some brandy in my cabinet in the saloon—if they've left us a bottle.'

Fleur found the drink-cabinet half empty, but a bottle of cognac had been left, and with this and a glass she returned to Blake's cabin. A stiff dose helped to pull him together. When she had found the first-aid box and dressed his wound, he looked more normal. The colour had returned to his face and he was breathing more evenly. Fleur had found peroxide and lint and with a pad managed to stem the flow of blood, before bandaging his head. She had a light, if inexperienced touch, but she managed well without causing him undue pain.

'Is that better?' she asked.

'Much,' he answered curtly. 'Now we must see what we can do about the yacht.'

Fleur nodded and sank into a chair and buried her face in her hands. She felt unnerved and wretched. The yacht was rocking badly in the swell of the sea, and a sudden crash of thunder shivered the glass in the porthole. A brilliant flash of lightning lit up Blake's disordered cabin. She looked up, startled. He was there standing near her, smoking a cigarette. He looked back at her grimly.

She said:

'It's getting worse.'

He nodded.

'And will probably continue to do so. Are you frightened?'

Her head shot up and she looked him full in the eyes now.

'No, I am not.'

'You will be, before you're through tonight.'

'Not of you,' she said, under her breath. 'You're wrong if you think *you* can scare me now. I don't care for storms at sea, but I prefer them, anyhow, to being touched by you.'

The man clenched his hands. For a moment he stood irresolute, staring at her. He had to admit she was brave. And deep in his heart he admired her. He felt sorry for her now. She looked so pathetically young crouching there in the chair in the wrecked cabin, her curls ruffled by the wind, her soft cheeks pale and tear-stained. She must, he knew, realise that this was no ordinary storm and that there was every likelihood of them coming near to death tonight. It seemed brutal to fight her and to make the whole atmosphere more sinister.

Only when he remembered that one word from her could have prevented it all did he harden his heart against her. Walking to the porthole, he stared out at the black sky. The weather certainly looked bad. Every now and then the lightning zigzagged across the clouds and lit up the angry sea.

He was turning to go up on deck when the door of the cabin was flung open and Benson came in. The officer looked spent and haggard.

'We're up against it now, sir,' he said. 'I've just got the wireless working. Italy has declared war against Great Britain.'

For a moment there was silence in the cabin. Then Blake whistled through his teeth.

'So that's it,' he said slowly. 'The blasted crew must have got wind of what was happening, and made away at the right moment.'

Benson nodded.

'What do we do now, sir? If we stay around here the Italians will probably send out a gunboat and take us in.'

'And chance being thrown up on the Italian coast and put in a concentration camp for the duration,' said Blake. 'No, thanks. I'm not fond of spaghetti.'

'What's the alternative?' Fleur asked hopelessly.

Ignoring her, Blake turned towards Benson. 'Where do you think we are?'

'I can't quite make out, sir,' the man replied. 'Drifting southwards, I think, into the very teeth of the gale. The storm should be at its height now. It's close on 2 a.m. If we can hold out for an hour or two, dawn will break and we should be able to get our bearings.'

Blake staggered as the ship rolled heavily, and supported himself against the side of the bed. When he spoke his voice was stern and authoritative.

'We'll get the engines started as soon as it eases up a bit,' he said. 'Then set a course due south. If we try to get into French territorial waters we might run into the Italian coastal patrol. If we're lucky we'll pick up with a convoy.'

'Shall I try sending a message?' Benson asked.

Blake shook his head.

'It might be intercepted. You had better get some food and drink now. You're going to need all your strength.'

'Very good, sir.'

As Benson went out, Fleur's eyes met Blake's, and she saw that they were full of grim determination. There was no trace of fear on his face. It was the face of a fighter who loved a fight.

'There you are,' he said to her. 'You see what you've mapped out for yourself. I don't suppose it'll be your idea of a pleasure cruise.'

'Preferable, anyhow, to your former plans for my entertainment,' she returned.

Crossing towards her, he suddenly flung away his cigarette and took her in his arms.

'So you think you're better off now? Well, we don't know what we're up against, but I intend to enjoy the next few hours to the full.'

'Do what you wish, as long as you don't expect me to share in your enjoyment.'

'But I do,' he said with a laugh. 'I haven't had any real excitement for months. This amuses me. A deserted yacht, with a beautiful woman who stood quietly by while the crew planned her ex-lover's early decease! It's fine! I should think it would appeal to the actress in you. Don't you think you owe me a lot of kisses for what you've done?'

'I hate you!'

'And *I* still want *you*!'

Fleur was never to forget the drama of the next few moments. Locked in Blake's arms, she was helpless. His lips were on hers. His face was a distorted mask, as white as the bandage she had bound around his head. Both of them swayed and staggered as the yacht rolled and pitched. Outside the thunder crashed on, and the wind rose to a howling screech.

Suddenly she felt the ship straining to meet a wave which hit the main-deck and bridge with a solid thud. There was the sound of breaking wood. The furniture was flung across the cabin with a series of crashes. Then she knew that she was falling backwards. There was a sudden tearing pain in the back of her head, a red flash before her eyes. In the distance the sound of Blake's voice calling her name—a voice which gradually faded out into a long silence.

CHAPTER EIGHT

It was always to be something of a mystery to Blake how, with Benson's help, he managed to survive the next few days.

The handling of the yacht, which was supposed to have a crew of eight, was killing work for the combined efforts of two men, neither of them fit. The engines alone were three men's work, and after some hours in the oppressive heat of the engine-room Blake found his heart was beginning to harass him, and was forced to hand over the job to Benson.

It was better for Blake on the bridge, where he could breathe fresh air and concentrate on navigation. Sleep was out of the question. During the long nights on watch he was almost too busy to think of rest. The unlighted ship had to be nursed every inch of the way—only when he went down to his cabin to snatch some food or drink did he feel an overpowering sense of fatigue.

Fleur was an added anxiety. The blow on the back of her head had resulted in slight concussion. There was nothing for her to do but lie still on her bed and wait for his periodic visits.

It had been obvious from the first that she would be unable to give any practical help to the two men. Her fall had been a bad one. It had given Blake a fright and helped to clear the mists of angry passion from his brain. After that mad storm had broken he had lifted her in his arms and carried her to the bed. Laying her down, he had unfastened her coat and moistened her lips with brandy from the bottle which she had brought for him.

Lying there with closed eyes, her long black lashes curving on the pallor of her cheeks, she has looked to him a helpless, lovely child, rather than the sophisticated woman of his distorted imagination. For an instant some of the old love and tenderness had flickered in Blake's heart. He could remember bending to kiss her hair.

'Fleur,' he had whispered. 'Why weren't you all that I thought you? Why did you have to break my dreams and my heart, when I loved you so?'

She did not stir. For a moment Blake hesitated, then had turned and left her alone. It was useless to force her back to consciousness. Better to let her sleep on, oblivious to her surroundings and what they must all go through before dawn.

In the early hours of that morning, Blake, on the bridge, watched the storm clear with the same rapidity with which it had begun. The sky became cloudless, the sea like a sheet of blue silk. The yacht was cutting through the smooth water now with steady ease.

Benson put his head around the corner of the engine-room door, and blinked at Blake in the strong light. He grinned as he wiped his face with an oily rag.

'Looking better now, sir,' he shouted towards the bridge. 'How are we going?'

Blake put down the chart which he had been studying, and leaned over the rail.

'Pretty well. It all depends on the weather. If our luck holds we should run into a convoy off the African coast. How's the fuel lasting out?'

Benson looked dubious. 'If we reduce speed, it may be all right. But I'd like to have some more.'

'Did you get any radio news?'

'Only propaganda stuff, sir. Trying to

suggest the possibility of the French capitulating.'

Blake found a cigarette and cupped his hands to light a match against the fresh morning breeze. He wished that he could be so sure that the talk of capitulation was merely enemy propaganda. There had been disturbing rumours current amongst the more reliable sources in Monte Carlo. Hints had been thrown out by more than one knowledgeable Frenchman—by Frenchmen who did not believe that a total war could not be won by an army sheltered behind the Maginot Line— which suggested that although the effect of military intervention by Italy would be slight, the moral effect would be overwhelming. Blake believed this opinion was held by the mass of the people, who showed none of their leaders' desire to escape from reality.

Blake himself was a realist. He loved and respected the French people, but if there was to be any chance of surrender he wanted to be as far away from the country as possible. He felt thankful that he had determined to make for the North African coast. The French colonies would be the last to consider capitulation. They would be able to refuel there, and take on a stock of food and drink before making for Gibraltar. It would be a long and dangerous journey, but it would be worth it. If Britain lost the use of the French fleet, it might mean that the Admiralty could be persuaded to find him some kind of a job.

The prospect of once again being of some use to his country kept him up during the next days when it became increasingly apparent from the wireless news that the French resistance was being broken.

Once he heard that the enemy had advanced round the flank of the Maginot Line, Blake knew that it was the beginning of the end. He cursed the name of the fatal *Ligne Maginot* which France had constructed to defend the nerves of her people. A false security had been planted on a nation of fighting men. It had drained the military initiative of the finest army in Europe. Its fall would cause panic and sap the morale of the people more surely than a dozen well-fought defeats on the battlefield.

He knew that the Italian thrust in the back must be the final nail in the coffin of a country which had begun to accept the fact that it was being beaten. It was a typical Italian gesture. Blake thought grimly of the crew which had managed to escape, and hoped that if he ever did manage to get back in the service, that he would be posted to the Mediterranean fleet.

The hope of future work and the fact that he had little time to think of his own petty troubles, caused a change in him which Fleur was quick to note. It was not until the third evening, when the fuel shortage became increasingly dangerous, that he showed any

116

signs of real anxiety.

He went down to Fleur's cabin and found her sitting up for the first time, drinking a strong cup of tea which she had made in the galley. She looked white and small and rather desolate, huddled in a fur cape. As Blake approached her bed her small face hardened. She was not very clear as to what had happened to her before that fall on to her head, but she knew vaguely that she had been defending herself against his brutality, she told herself, no pity because *he* looked strained and pale.

'It's the very devil,' he said. 'We can't be more than a few miles from the coast. Another night would have got us there.'

'How much longer can we go on?' she asked.

'It's impossible to say, it mostly depends on the weather. I don't like the look of that sky.'

She shivered.

'You mean there's a chance of another storm?'

'More than a chance. I'd like to bet we're running into hell's own weather. I'm going back to the bridge.'

His prediction was correct. During the hours of darkness the waves began to rise to an ever-increasing wind. The yacht, nosing her way at a reduced speed through the trough of the sea, shuddered painfully against the swell.

The bridge became a soaking square of

water. Blake, his eyes dazzled by vivid streaks of lightning, peered across the dark expanse of water. They must, he decided, be dangerously near land. A moment later he became aware of a great shadowy mass which seemed to loom towards the ship at an alarming speed. He was right! They had reached what appeared to be a cluster of rocks leading out from the shore. It was too late to try to turn the yacht away. There was nothing to do except to get hold of the others and make a dash for it.

Running down the ladder from the bridge, he wrenched open the door of the wireless-cabin where Benson sat with a pair of headphones to his ears.

'Is anything wrong, sir?' the officer asked, looking up from the instrument panel to see Blake's tense face.

'Plenty!' snapped Blake. 'We're drifting on to some rocks.'

'Rocks!' Benson repeated. 'But we must be miles from the shore.'

'Don't be a fool, man. The gale has been directing our course inland. You can see a whole line of cliffs standing out alone in the sea. We don't want to be on the yacht if she hits them. Can you get three lifebelts?'

'Yes, sir. You mean to jump for it?'

'Exactly.'

'What about Miss Lorraine?'

'I'll get her now,' Blake returned. 'Meet me

aft on the upper deck.'

Fleur had dressed and was in her cabin smoking a cigarette, trying to smooth her jangled nerves. Blake flung open the door and as he saw her his thoughts were no longer revengeful or bitter. His only idea was to protect and save her. Whatever she had done, she was a woman, and he loved her passionately. He would not tolerate the thought of that radiant beauty, that grace and youth being swamped and broken against the rocks.

'Come along,' he said gently—more gently than he had spoken for days. 'We're moving.'

'What do you mean? Moving where?'

'You'll see for yourself in a moment. For heaven's sake do what I tell you and don't ask questions. It's a matter of life and death now.'

She followed him obediently. Reaching the deck, they found Benson struggling with one of the lifeboats. Blake strapped a lifebelt about Fleur and one around himself. She could see practically nothing through the black pall of the storm. The howling of the gale and the crackling of thunder drowned her voice when she tried to gasp out a question.

It seemed an eternity before the small boat was finally set on the water and she was lowered by Benson and caught in Blake's arms. The boat plunged and rolled on the mountainous waves. The yacht seemed to reel and tower above them like a white giant, waiting in the darkness to crush them.

Suddenly Fleur heard a broken shout from Blake.

'*Mind*, Benson! Look out, man! Wait a moment!'

Then a monster wave engulfed them and Fleur found herself struggling in the sea. Cold, relentless water was filling her lungs and choking her. It was the second time since leaving Monte Carlo that she was to experience all the horrors of drowning, but this time her lifebelt kept her up and saved her. When a brilliant flash of lightning lit up the waters around her, she caught a glimpse of Blake clinging to the boat which had overturned and was floating with its keel in the air.

'Can you get to this boat?' he yelled.

She gasped.

'I think so!'

She was not more than a few yards from it. A few desperate strokes brought her alongside. When she felt Blake's arms around her she gave a choking gasp:

'I can't go on.'

'Of course you can,' he shouted back. 'You must. Force yourself to keep going.'

'I'll try.'

'Then follow me, when I give the word. Hold on to the boat for a bit. The storm is settling down. We're close in to the rocks. We should make land pretty easily. Can you see?'

She strained her water-filled eyes and saw what he indicated. There was a gradual rift in the blackness of the sky. The first streak of pink and amber from the east. Dawn was breaking and now she could make out the line of the shore. Rocks seemed to be within comparatively easy distance. Yes, she felt certain that she could get there. Then she thought of Blake and wondered if his heart would stand the strain.

It was growing lighter every moment. Silhouetted against the sky, she saw a cluster of palms swaying in the wind. Behind them the yacht was drifting towards the headland. The gale was dying down and very soon the sky became a light grey.

Fleur's hands were numb with cold, her muscles drawn with the pain of clinging to the upturned boat.

'Can we go now?' she cried.

Blake nodded.

'Make for that rock between the palms. I'll try to keep alongside you.'

Striking out with a powerful breast-stroke in the direction he indicated, Fleur did not stop until she felt solid ground beneath her feet. For a few minutes she lay in the shallow water gasping for breath, then turned round to look out to sea.

Blake was near her, but obviously exhausted. He was about twenty yards from the shore, almost motionless, his head half-submerged, his arms moving feebly. It was apparent to her that his heart was failing him.

Wading out in the water, she called:

'This way, Blake. You're just there.'

Her voice seemed to rouse him to further effort. Turning on his side, he half raised his head and made a few spasmodic strokes which brought him to her side.

Stooping down, she put her hands under his shoulders and pulled him towards the sand, where he lay pale and motionless. She began to chafe his hands anxiously. In this unforgettable moment all animosity was forgotten. She was afraid that he might die. But Blake's pulse-beats were stronger now and his breathing returned. He made an effort to sit up and speak to her.

'Where's Benson?'

Fleur scanned the blue expanse of water.

'God knows! There's no sign of him.'

Blake closed his eyes.

'I thought as much. He jumped too soon. I think he got caught between the yacht and the boat.'

'Oh, my God, are you sure?'

He nodded.

'I'm afraid so, poor devil. Poor old Benson. He was a grand chap.'

'It's horrible,' she said, shuddering, 'horrible.'

Simultaneously the man and the girl sat up and stared around them. The stretch of land which jutted out to sea seemed like a strangely beautiful little island, lying like a jewel in the blue Mediterranean. Great feathery trees, date-palms and flowering bushes grew along the shore. There was no sign of human habitation. The land looked as though it were a primitive spot untouched by civilisation.

The dawn had broken; the storm was over and sea and land were bathed in warm, amber light as the sun rose high in the heavens.

Fleur and Blake, sighing deeply, turned to each other. He looked haggard and spent, the wet bandages clinging to his forehead, his once immaculate suit torn to shreds. She was a slim, shivering figure in a soaked dress which was clinging to her knees.

The man spoke first, in a strange, quiet voice:

'Do you realise what has happened, Fleur?'

'I don't want to think,' she whispered, and sank back on the sand and buried her face on the curve of her arm. 'I feel absolutely done.'

He sat down beside her and put a hand on her quivering shoulder. There was a queer exultant look in his eyes.

'We're on some part of the Algerian coast,' he said. 'Probably east of Oran, but I can only guess at that. Anyhow, it's deserted and it looks as though we're going to see a lot of each other—*toute seule*—in the immediate future.'

For a moment, Fleur did not answer. She was, as she told Blake, feeling done and exhausted. She had but one consolation—that they were on warm sand, where it appeared to be comparatively safe and agreeable in comparison with the cold terror which she had experienced in the sea.

As the hot sun rose higher she ceased to shiver, and sat still, staring before her. A yellow light spread across a sky of inviolate blue. The wind had dropped. Not a breath stirred the tall palms or the tamarisks fringing the shore. Both Blake and Fleur were bone-dry now. Their bodies and brains, which had been numb with exhaustion and the horror of the recent hour, gradually thawed and became normal. They felt themselves once again becoming human beings, who were able to think and act and speak with some semblance of intelligence.

Fleur lay back on the sand and shut her eyes. Blake raised his head and drew a long, deep breath. He looked up at the dazzling beauty of the sky, and the radiant freshness of the morning on this unknown part of the land which harboured them, and felt that it was good to be alive. He drew his hand away from Fleur's shoulder, then crossing both arms about his knees, raised his face to the sun and shut his eyes.

She opened hers and looked at him.

'Is your head all right?'

'More or less. I'm enjoying this sun. Aren't you?'

She nodded. She was indeed refreshed after a long, quiet spell. But her limbs ached and her eyes felt red and sore from the salt water. She wished that she had Blake's power of recuperation and his optimistic fatalism. She was not at all sure that she was glad to be alive. She was still suffering from reaction, and could share little of his enthusiasm for life.

She put a hand to her hair. It was dry, but to her it felt sticky and tangled. She had no mirror, no make-up, she knew that she must be looking her worst. Face unpowdered, nose shiny, dress no more than a tattered rag. She thought longingly of her bag with its flapjack, lipstick, and all the familiar accessories.

Blake seemed to be ignoring her existence. He was still sitting with his head flung back, his eyes shut and a rapt expression on his face. The sun beat down upon him. He was, she knew, first and foremost a creature of the sun, and his appearance caused her a fleeting moment of jealousy. He did not look as though his heart had almost failed him. He was brown and glowing, his thick black hair showed smooth and shining where the bandage did not hide it. None the worse for the sea-water and the lack of a brush. His lips had lost that blue tinge. Even in his crumpled suit he did not look ridiculous. She wished that she could share his aptitude for appearing so coolly collected in an emergency.

She surveyed their surroundings with frank

gloom. What part of the coast was this? How far was the nearest village or town? She had to admit the sheer beauty of the scene before them. The radiant sea was no longer angry and terrifying as it had been last night. It rippled like emerald and blue silk; little creamy waves lapping the long line of gold virgin sand.

Behind them were a few palms and flowering shrubs. Seagulls flew overhead crying shrilly. A fat puffin hopped beside them, staring at them with beady, inquisitive eyes. There was no sign of a living soul or human dwelling. Even the ill-fated yacht had disappeared behind the rocks, without so much as the sign of a mast to show where she had lain before she sank.

'We shall starve and die,' Fleur thought hopelessly. 'That's what will happen to us.'

Aloud, she said:

'Don't you think we'd better discuss what we're going to do? We can't sit about sunbathing for the rest of the day.'

'Up to the moment you haven't been exactly communicative yourself,' was his quick reply. 'I asked you whether you realised that we don't know where we are, or what you think we can do about it. We may have to stay here alone for weeks—or months.'

'Not if I can help it,' Fleur said bluntly. The colour rose to her pale cheeks, and stayed in a deep burning red which crept to the roots of her hair and down to her slender throat. 'Why, it's *fantastic*. We left France less than a week ago—this place can't be the end of the earth— a desert island.'

Blake hunched his shoulders.

'Columbus may have said the same when he discovered America. It does sound fantastic, but facts are facts. Here we are! It's a little-known part of the map, although it may be quite near civilisation. The best thing to do is to explore. Come along. Feeling strong enough?'

'I think so.'

He jumped to his feet and stretched his arms above his head. Fleur glanced at him sulkily, and he gave her a quick, questioning look. The ghost of a smile—the smile of the old cynical Blake—curved his hard mouth.

'You look annoyed, my dear. I admit it must be hard for you to play the part of the castaway, but you'll just have to make the best of it.'

'I won't,' she said, with a sudden burst of anger. 'I won't.'

'Then what *will* you do?'

'I don't know. But it's certain we can't stay here for the rest of our lives.'

'It doesn't look too bad to me.'

'Well, to me it looks ghastly.'

He laughed.

'I know what's troubling you. You've got no clothes, no powder, no brush and comb. Just a film-set, but no publicity manager. Isn't that it?'

Fleur clenched her teeth.

'Don't be so stupid,' she flashed.

Tears of sheer rage had come into her eyes. There were times when she really hated this man whom once she had loved. Hated his brutal, direct truths. It was typical of him to say a thing like that. To strip one mentally and expose all one's lesser artificialities and petty little desires. He was so blatantly sincere.

Blake indeed felt sincere in this fresh, brilliant morning after his recent experiences. He felt primitive man, with primitive instincts. He was at one with the beauty of the scene around him, and had no desire for affectation or pretence. He was here on this barren strip of Algerian coast, with a woman whom he had once loved and still desired. A woman whom he considered had done him a grievous wrong. It was up to her to face the position in which they found themselves. She also must do away with pretence. She would have to learn to accept and cope with any eventuality which might arise.

He held out a hand.

'Get up and come with me.'

His authoritive voice and manner infuriated her.

'Don't order me about like that,' she said.

For answer he leaned down and, gripping her hand, pulled her to her feet.

'You are not a princess, my dear. That is all

over, and we are not in the Sporting Club now. You're going to do what I say.'

'You're wrong,' she said. 'You'll find that out for yourself.'

The tears ran down her face. Blake thought she had never looked more beautiful than at this moment with those angry, scarlet cheeks, and great angry eyes. The lack of powder and paint pleased him. She was unaffected and natural. He even liked her torn ragged dress, showing every line of her superb figure. Her silk stockings were in shreds. She was lucky enough, he thought, to be wearing sandal shoes with flat heels. It would make walking easy for her.

'We're not going to argue now,' he said. 'I don't know about you, but I'm hungry. I suggest we look for some food.'

She wiped her tears away with the back of her hand, like a child.

'Where do we find it? Have you a favourite restaurant here?'

Blake smiled surlily and began to walk over the beach. She followed him reluctantly. They went a long way down the golden sands, meeting only seabirds who were tame and unafraid, as though they had never come in contact before with such strange creatures, and had not learned to fear them.

He eyed her dubiously. The faintest expression of amusement lay in his eyes. He took hold of her hand.

'It's a queer bit of land,' remarked Blake, 'I'm ready to bet it's uninhabited for miles around. We'd better try going inland for a bit.'

'It's beastly walking with this dress clinging round my legs,' Fleur protested.

'Come along, don't worry about your appearance,' he told her. 'If your dress is difficult to walk in, pull it up and fix it round your waist. It doesn't matter what you look like. There's nobody to see you except myself and the birds—and we don't care.'

'My shoes hurt.'

'Then take them off.'

'You're very kind,' she said sullenly, 'but walking without them might be even more painful.'

'This is hardly the time for social conventions,' said Blake. 'We may be up against anything in this place. If I were you I should dispense with your petty civilised likes and dislikes. Take the shoes off. Carry them or throw them away. I'm going to do the same. The earth looks good enough to walk on.'

He let go of her hand and removing his shoes, tied the laces together and slung them over his arm. Then taking off his coat and crumpled shirt and collar, he stood before her, neck and chest brown and bare to the sun.

She suddenly remembered his head wound.

'Shall I undo your bandage?' she suggested. 'It must be sticking and uncomfortable.'

He nodded.

'Thanks. I wish you would. The cut those swine gave me will heal better if it gets the air. The salt water will have done nothing but good.'

Her heart softened towards him when he knelt in front of her and lifted his bandaged head. She took the dressing off gently. He winced when she had to tear it from the wound, but smiled his thanks. The cut looked as though it was healing, the bruise was less discoloured.

'Is that better?' she asked.

'Much. Now for some food. You must be starving.'

She had to admit that she was hungry.

'I am,' she said. 'But the prospect hardly looks cheerful.'

'We'll see what we can do,' he answered quite gaily. 'You'd better learn not to expect too much, then you won't be disappointed. My island princess can't expect the Hôtel de Paris *cuisine*.'

Her colour deepened. She tossed her head and tried to laugh.

'Say all the beastly things you want—I can take it.'

'Then we'll get on splendidly.'

She realised that he was incorrigible; still scornful and determined to master her. A wave of silent despair seized her as she walked beside him. He went ahead swiftly and gracefully on his bare feet, and she found it hard to keep up with him. Blake, the sophisticated man of the world, seemed to her a born explorer—a man who loved nature in the raw. He was terrifically complex, she decided, and incomprehensible. They went further inland towards a thick tangle of trees and bushes. The trees were tall and shady here with luxuriant foliage. She did not know their names. There were olives, delicately pale and shimmering like silver in the sunlight. Climbing vines and flowering plants were fringed around little clearances which might have been fairy dells of enchanting loveliness. They found a wood full of birds and squirrels which looked like a part of England, but most of the country was purely Eastern with an exotic, languorous atmosphere.

When they had explored for a mile or two Blake was frankly mystified and Fleur thoroughly dispirited and dragging at his side like a tired child. She was finally forced to take off her shoes and stockings and tie her dress around her waist. She looked like a boy—a boy with long slim legs and bare curly head. She was nearly crying with fatigue and discouragement when they suddenly came upon a mass of fruit and nuts.

They seemed to be in a natural orange-grove and here grew a variety of trees: passion-fruit and firm, oily nuts which tasted like Brazils and were excellent to eat. They finished with drinks of pure crystal water from a brook which ran through the wood on the fringe of the headland.

'This place is a puzzle,' Blake said, when he had finished his meal. 'It isn't like anything I've ever seen before. If I didn't know we were in Africa I'd be hard put to say where we were. I bet we're the first people to have been here for a great many years.'

'I suppose so,' said Fleur.

'Let's call it Ruritania,' he suggested with a smile. 'You can be the Balkan princess here to your heart's content.'

She bit her lip and turned from him.

'Don't you think you ride that business to death? Do you never get tired of it?'

'You didn't get tired when you were enjoying your publicity stunt in Monte Carlo,' he retaliated. 'This is my turn.'

'How often have I to tell you that I'm sorry for that deception? I really did regret it, but now I'm tired of hearing about it. God knows you've never let me forget—' She broke off suddenly and buried her face in her arms. 'This is a grand prospect for me—stuck here with you! It's an impossible position.'

'You're making the worst of it,' he suggested. 'Personally, I'm not hating it or anything else. I'm rather glad to leave finances and all the artificialities of the world behind, and take to the simple life—with you!'

She made no reply. There seemed little to say, until he flung himself at her side and

133

circled her with his arms.

She shrank away from him.

'You can't expect me to share your pleasures,' she told him bitterly.

'Why not? Why not forget our quarrels and misunderstandings? They belong to the civilised past. We're primitive man and woman now. I'll fish and trap birds for food which you can cook. We can be completely free, obeying only our natural instincts. It could be grand fun. Real life, which neither of us has ever known. Why not enjoy it? Forget about trivialities—your future career and ambitions— and be yourself.'

'I *am* myself,' she replied, straining away from him. 'You've deliberately misunderstood and misjudged me all the way along. I'm not the cheap sensationalist you thought me. But it's no good arguing. If I've got to stay in this outlandish place with you—then I've got to. But I won't enjoy it. I won't be mastered by you or any other man. I shall merely exist until some ship passes or we can find the road which leads back to civilisation.'

His arms tightened about her.

'That was quite a long speech for a castaway princess but it's nonsense. You belong to me now. There's a delightful lack of rivals for your hand. It's time you acknowledged the fact.'

'I won't,' she said. 'You can believe that.'

He tried to reach her lips, but suddenly she pushed him back and springing up, darted away. She ran like one demented, like a frightened nymph being pursued by a satyr, straight into the woods from which they had just come.

Blake jumped up and followed. His eyes were shining. This was playing into his hands. It was primitive and exciting. A breathless chase—the woman fleeing, the man pursuing, eager-eyed and determined to conquer.

Fleur stumbled over a carpet of roots and stones. Twice she tripped and nearly fell, but regaining her breath, ran on panting and flushed. She came out of the little wood into the sunlight and found herself on the shore facing the sea. She raced on headlong towards the water as though eager to fling herself into the waves and swim away from the man who pursued her.

Blake was there before she reached the glittering margin of the water. Flinging both arms around her, he drew her back, pressing her hot, flushed face against his own.

'I enjoyed that, my little Fleur. You can't tell me you hate me, that you really want to get away from me!'

She felt exhausted and defeated. She was so tired that she could hardly stand. For a brief moment she struggled, then went limp in his arms. She felt his kisses, warm and demanding, on her mouth and eyes. Against her will she knew the overpowering thrill of that moment, and the fierce thrill of capture. He was winning the first round of the battle. As they stood together on the fringe of the sea with the hot sun beating down on them, she had to make a superhuman effort to continue the struggle.

She tried to speak and protest, but no speech came. She was too overcome with physical and mental fatigue to want to argue. Her head sank on his shoulder, and he heard her give a little cry:

'Blake—I can't stand any more . . .'

The pathos of her seemingly complete surrender, of her sheer accessibility, cooled the passion which had been flaming in him. He loved and despised her. Hated and wanted her. He didn't know what he felt. His reactions were chaotic, and for a moment he was defeated—by her defeat. He felt surprised that he was still unable to think along a straight course. There were so many more vital and important things to be considered that he felt it ludicrous to dwell on this one subject. He wondered why this girl, Fleur Lorraine, should have such a devastating effect of his mind and body.

He picked her up in his arms and carried her back to the shade of the trees. He laid her down on the warm sand.

'Stay there and get some sleep,' he said. 'It's what you want more than anything else.'

She did not answer, but shut her eyes and pillowed her face against her arm. For a long time he sat beside her, his brooding eyes staring across the sunlit sea. Through force of habit he fumbled in his pockets for cigarettes, and found that his case had not let in the water. His gold petrol-lighter still worked.

'Thank heavens for that,' he said to himself, and drew a long, satisfying breath of tobacco.

When he looked at Fleur again she was asleep. She lay still and breathing heavily, as though utterly tired out. He studied her tear-stained face, the curling lashes and half-open mouth, and cursed inwardly.

This position was sheer, unmitigated hell. For once in his life he could have been completely happy. He was cut off from the superficialities of the world he had known, and where ill-health had prevented him from playing his part in the world war. This barren stretch of land might have been his own particular Utopia had Fleur been different. Perhaps he had only himself to blame, he thought. He had been hard and ruthless. He knew it. And if she had been of different calibre, if she had been a sophisticated and worldly woman of his own set, he would have known how to deal with her.

He had loved her. He could love her even now. But she had used her youth and beauty to trick and make a fool of him. How could he forget that? He was determined that he should not become her slave again, that he should not let that same youth and beauty move him to pity or cajole him into giving her her own way.

Why should he? She was here alone with him—so very much alone—and he could take her completely for his own. He could not let her cheat him for a second time.

When Fleur awoke it was late in the afternoon. She found that Blake had been busy. He had gathered sticks—there was a large heap of them in front of a glowing fire. She was astonished to see that a fish was cooking in the middle of the embers. In the shade of the tree were two ripe coco-nut shells full of sweet, cool milk for them to drink.

Blake, himself, appeared to be in a more amiable mood. He did not begin by jeering or dictating to her. He was more like the charming and thoughtful man whom she had known and loved in Monte Carlo.

'Let me give you your breakfast in bed,' he said gaily, and laughed.

'I've been asleep,' she said, rubbing her eyes.

'You certainly have. For several hours without a murmur. Now you must eat my meal. Breakfast, tea, supper—I'm not quite sure what to call it. I've no idea what the time is, but it must be late afternoon according to the position of the sun. Have some of this fish—it smells good.'

Fleur nodded her head. She felt quiet and subdued by the thought of his fierce capture and the embrace to which she had been forced to yield some hours ago.

'It looks good,' she said. 'How on earth did you get it?'

'I used to catch trout in the river at home, when I was a boy,' Blake answered. 'You lie on the bank and scoop them out of the pools with your hands. I don't know what these fellows call themselves, but they taste like Dover soles.'

Fleur found the fish excellent. They both ate ravenously, tearing the flesh with their fingers. After the meal, Fleur collected the bones and threw them into the woods.

'That was fine,' she said. 'Really, my dear Blake, you are a modern Robinson Crusoe.'

'Which reminds me,' he answered. 'Today is Friday. What a grand idea for a film! "The Woman Friday", starring Fleur Lorraine. There's your publicity! I'll sell it to Manton when I see him.'

Fleur ignored this piece of sarcasm. It was the first time since the yachting disaster that he had mentioned Mark's name. She was again conscious of the bitterness in his voice. To her the word 'film' recalled the studios at Balham, the old job and her mother and Betty, Mark Manton and her reign as Princess in Monte Carlo. It all seemed so strangely far away. Like another life on another planet.

The last radio-news which they had received on the yacht had told them of the breaking up of the French war effort. It was unbearable to think of the all-shattering events which were taking place in that world which they had left, and not to know what had happened to those they loved.

She thought of her grandfather's reactions to France's surrender. Dear grandpa, who always used to speak of the French Army as Europe's first and last line of defence. Now the Germans would concentrate the whole weight of their power against England. Perhaps London had already known the terrors of aerial bombardment. She remembered their cheaply built house in Streatham Hill, but was thankful that they had a deep cellar. And little Betty, who worked in an office near the docks, she would undoubtedly be in the danger zone.

Mark Manton, she knew, would probably have forgotten Fleur Lorraine's very existence in his rush for safety, and she could not resist a secret feeling of exultation when she thought of him panicking towards an air-raid shelter. How he must be regretting the publicity-stunt which had been begun with so much hope of profitable success! How he would enjoy commercialising her present position, which put any of his professional schemes into abeyance! If she ever got back to England she would have a story to tell which would shake the studios to their depths. *If she ever got back!*

'Blake,' she said, 'tell me candidly what you think of our chances.'

'Of being found?' he asked.

'Yes. What do we sit here and wait for?'

140

He shrugged his shoulders.

'So much depends on Benson. He may have radioed an S O S before we abandoned the yacht. In which case we may get picked up at any moment. Why do you ask?'

'It's pretty obvious, isn't it? I don't exactly share your love of wide open spaces and nature in the raw. Apart from any personal feelings I may have, there are my family and friends to think about.'

Blake stared out at the horizon. He could see the outline of a ship passing slowly along. It looked to him as though it might be a thousand miles away.

'It's possible,' he said, pointing towards it, 'that a boat may come near to land, or a 'plane may fly overhead. We'll build a bonfire on the highest part of the hill and light it if we see any chance of attracting attention. But I don't expect that will be for some time.'

'I don't suppose it will,' she said under her breath.

The rest of the day passed strangely. Both of them avoided personal discussions, conversing mostly about the country and how they would exist if they were left for many days in exile. Blake caught more fish, and Fleur gathered a quantity of fruit and nuts with which they managed to assuage their hunger. By night time they both felt tired by the sun and fresh air but completely recovered from the effects of their terrible experience of the day before.

When darkness fell and the beach was bathed in moonlight and a glory of stars bejewelled the sky, there arose the question of where they should sleep. It was a thing about which Fleur had thought several times, but she had not mentioned it to Blake. She was glad when he, himself, broached it.

Blake looked at her. She was a strange unreal figure in her torn dress, with her boyish head of tangled curls. The moonlight gave her an almost ethereal look. The whole lonely country was drenched in light. It seemed a white gleaming romantic world created for love and lovers. The beauty of it gripped him by the throat. When he spoke his voice was tense.

'You'll have to sleep on the dry sand, under the palms,' he said. 'I'll cover you with my coat. I'm afraid it's the best I can do for you.'

'I'll be all right,' she answered quickly. 'I can look after myself.'

Suddenly he moved towards her, and she could see that passion was sweeping him again like a tempest, on this warm night of bewildering sweetness. He caught her in his arms and put his cheek against hers. He was not master now, but lover. A lover weakening her resolve to hate and fight him.

'Fleur,' he whispered, 'let me look after you. Just for tonight. This is our own enchanted land. We are enchanted. Let my shoulder be a pillow for your lovely head, let my arms shield you from the night-wind. Don't turn from me, Fleur. Love me . . . *love me tonight* . . .'

She shut her eyes for a moment, breathless with excitement, with fear and with passion. All the emotions in the world seemed to sweep her up and drown her. Blake saying such things! Blake holding her so close to his heart, pleading for her love! This was the Blake she had adored and had, indeed, loved devotedly on that night on the moonlit terrace at Monte Carlo. She found it infinitely difficult to struggle against him—to be practical and proud—all the things she ought to be. Yet something deep down in her whispered through the tempest of emotion, saying:

'Don't give in. You will regret it and so will he. Don't give in . . .'

She listened to that small inner voice. She knew it was right. If she surrendered to the witchery of this night and gave herself up to the magic of her lover's passion, she would never be able to hold her head up again. He would have every right in future to despise her and think her weak and foolish. And he, himself, in the clear light of morning, would have a bitter taste in his mouth. She must gain control. She must be strong, and prove by her very strength that her love for him was real and deep. That it could rise above the lure of passion.

'You must be crazy!' she said, struggling in

his arms. 'You don't know what you're saying.'

'Crazy perhaps,' he said wildly. 'Crazy with love for you. You may as well know the truth. I can't hate you. I've tried it, and it just won't work. I can't despise you for what you've done. I can only want and adore you with every fibre of my being. I can only think of you and say "I love you. Be kind to me. Love me as you did that night in France".'

'That's finished and over with,' she gasped. 'You know it is. Let me go now. Please let me go.'

She opened her eyes and he saw that they were glittering with tears, tears which welled over and ran down her cheeks. He hesitated. With one hand he smoothed back a silky wave of hair from her forehead. He kissed her on the lips.

'Can't you forget the past, and live for the present? Darling, only you and I are here—alone—under the stars.'

With a quick wrench she tore herself forcibly away from him. Her cheeks were like blazing poppies. She trembled violently.

'I will *not* forget. You must be mad to pretend you love me after all your brutality and spite. Do you think I could ever believe in your love again now or at any other time? Of course not!'

He was sobered. For an instant he stood staring at her, breathing jerkily. He found it difficult not to draw her back against his body

144

and hold her there. He wanted to hide his hot face against her cool white shoulder and feel her arms around his neck. But something imperative, decisive in her tone, defeated him. He bit his lip and his handsome head went down. He avoided looking at her.

'Very well, Fleur. If you don't believe I really care . . .'

'How can I?' she broke out, half crying. 'Ever since you carried me off in that absurd fashion, you have bullied me and tortured me with your childish sneers and jibes.'

'You drove me to it,' he said. 'I was angry— I've always admitted it—half demented with anger because you tricked me with that damnable princess business. I meant to punish you—to get even with you.'

'Which you did,' she reminded him bitterly. 'Without pausing for one moment to ask yourself whether I was really to blame; or whether it had just happened, unfortunately, that we grew to care for each other while I was acting a part for the company which employed me. You never gave me the benefit of the doubt. You simply took it for granted that I had wilfully deceived you.'

He looked up at her, doubt and confusion in his mind. She spoke so earnestly, so honestly. How could he doubt that, at least, she was being honest now? Had he wronged her? Had he been too prejudiced, too ready to believe that she had never loved him genuinely?

'You're trying to alter my feelings, to make me out a fool who has blundered badly,' he muttered, 'but I'm not altogether a brute and a beast. Remember, when we first met at Monte Carlo, I adored you. I thought of you with deepest respect and admiration as my future wife. I was prepared to give or offer you all that which I had never wished to give any other woman in my life.'

'Because you thought me a princess with some kind of a title behind me,' Fleur cried, her eyes blazing through the tears. 'As soon as you knew I was an unknown actress, you changed your mind. You decided I wasn't good enough to marry.'

'That's a lie, Fleur. You've no right to say that.' Blake was angry now. His face livid. 'I would have cared for you if you'd been in rags—the lowliest creature on earth—as long as I thought you genuine, and truly in love with me. You don't imagine that all I was wanting was a title?'

'And why not?'

'Don't be a fool,' he snapped. 'It was the deceit, the bluff which infuriated me. And Manton. Don't forget I heard him say you were hand in glove with him—that you intended to marry him once the stunt was over.'

'And you believed him, Blake?'

'Yes,' he said, his brows puckered. 'I did.'

'So much for your faith in me.'

He brought one clenched hand down on the other.

'You can't turn the tables on me like this, making me out to be the transgressor and yourself the injured innocent. I won't have it, my dear.'

'Neither will I stand here and listen to you protesting that you adore me after all you've recently done and said,' she said stonily. 'You're just a mass of selfishness and egotism. You want what is hard to get and I refuse to give way.'

They faced each other, hands clenched, faces white with rage and accusation, muscles taut. They were not lovers now, but enemies fighting for their rights. For a full minute they stared at each other. Fleur felt indignant and determined not to surrender to this man who had bullied and hurt her. Blake felt equally indignant and determined not to let her put all the blame upon him. Neither would relent.

Fleur sat down on the warm earth and drew a hand across her eyes and face.

'For heaven's sake go! Leave me alone,' she said wearily. 'I'm tired out—sick of all this.'

His heart seemed to turn over and ache with sudden love and pity. He felt a tenderness in which there was no passion. He dropped down on one knee beside her, and touched her bent curly head with his hand.

'Fleur,' he said huskily, 'my dear, don't cry. Please don't cry. I'm damned sorry for

147

everything. You make me feel such a swine.'

'Which is exactly what you are.'

'Fleur!' he protested. 'Be fair . . .'

'I've been fair. I told you I deceived you, but not with any definite desire to trick you into loving me. I am not and never was what you appear to think me. You didn't give me a chance to tell you the truth—and I hate you for it.'

He stared at her miserably. He was fast losing his own sense of importance and righteous anger against her. Fast feeling that he had been too hasty in his judgment. But what could he say? What could he do now, after all that he had done? She was certainly right. He had been brutally hard, even though he was under the impression that she was deserving the punishment which he served out.

A sickening sensation that he had blundered badly and lost all chance of winning Fleur's love rushed over him. He sat down on the earth beside her and put his dark boyish head on the curve of her arm.

'What a mess!' he said wearily. 'What a hell of a mess!'

She glanced at him, and wiped the tears from her eyes with the back of one slim hand. She also was fast losing her sense of righteousness. She was, she felt, only a tired and rather frightened girl who had been through a series of shattering experiences and who had had a gruelling day. And to make matters worse, she loved this man. Yes, loved him. She might declare that she hated him with her last breath, but deep in her heart she knew that she cared, and had cared since the hour in Monte Carlo when he had first held her in his arms and laid one rapturous, unforgettable kiss upon her lips.

Pride battled with this love. She wanted to turn to him, to fling herself into his arms now, at this very moment, and say, 'Blake, darling, take me . . . I love you . . . forget the past . . . nothing matters!' But she could not. There were things that mattered more than love or passion. First of all came pride and self-respect. If she gave in to Blake now—and in to herself— she would lose his self-respect for ever.

She said in a muffled voice:

'It's no use going on like this, Blake. We won't get any further. You'd better leave me— let me sleep.'

He looked at her.

'Fleur,' he said, 'I don't know what to say— what to do. You've somehow revolutionised my feelings tonight. My whole outlook is changed. You've made me feel frankly ashamed.'

'Don't,' she answered. 'There's no need for apologies on either side. It seems we have both made mistakes. Only go away. I'm so tired. I can't go on unless I have some rest.'

Her weary little voice hurt him intolerably. He would have given a fortune to be able to fling himself down beside her and lay his head against her shoulder. He loathed himself now for his passion, his cruel punishment of her. What right had he to condemn! He was no plaster saint. Who was he that he should take it upon himself to become her judge and jury!

He was overwhelmed with remorse, and cursed himself bitterly for what he had done in the blindness of his rage. Somehow he believed in Fleur. He felt that she was honest—that she had always been honest. The princess business had obviously never been a calculated act on her part to trick him. Of that he was convinced. And she said that Mark Manton had lied about their relationship to each other. He could even believe that now. It was her word against Manton's.

There seemed little he could do or say at the moment to show Fleur that he was sorry. She was too tired and unhappy. He felt it impossible to force any kind of scene upon her this evening. It would be better to leave her, as she asked. Tomorrow he would tell her what he felt—how much he loved her—how much he wanted her forgiveness.

He got up and drew a hand across his eyes.

'I'll find a place not far away. You'd better stay here and try to get some sleep. Good night, Fleur. I feel dumb—speechless. I can't begin to tell you all that I feel.'

'Thank you.'

It was on the tip of her tongue to tell him

not to leave her, not to go away. She would have given much to feel his arms about her, comforting her; his kisses reassuring her of his love. But she said no more.

'You are sure you'll be all right? You will manage to get some rest?' he asked.

'Quite all right.'

Fleur lay down like a weary child under a palm tree which shaded her from the brilliant moonlight. Behind her lay the mysterious beauty of North Africa. Before her, the starlit loveliness of the rippling sea.

Blake leaned down and covered her with his coat. He bit hard at his lip. It seemed incredible to him in this moment that he could ever have felt a desire to sneer at or hurt her. He could have cried—cried like a child and asked her pardon. But he was dumb. They were both silently awkward and embarrassed in the face of the first real understanding and explanation that had arisen between them.

After a moment he went away. She watched him go, glancing through her fingers which covered her eyes. Her heart throbbed and ached. Once again she had to force herself to be quiet.

The tall figure disappeared through the feathery trees, and she wondered half-heartedly where he had gone and what he would do. She felt so alone, so miserable without him. The woods suddenly grew sinister and full of ominous shadows. There was no sound save the lapping of the waves on the shore. She felt cold and nervous. Instinctively she sat up and called out:

'Blake . . .'

Her voice was lost in the vastness of the night. It was lost to the man who strode slowly along through the woods, trying to build up the wreckage of love and passion which seemed to him all that was left of the once glorious dream of a princess in Monte Carlo.

CHAPTER NINE

There was another man whose thoughts had been centred almost entirely upon Fleur during the last days of France's struggle.

Mark Manton, lounging in the heat of a June morning on the steps of the British Consulate at Cannes, looked with apparent distaste at the crowd which surged over the Croisette.

He was a much mystified and furious Manton. For the last few days he had known little peace of mind or body, had drunk too much, eaten practically no food and spent hour after hour trying in vain to find some clue which might lead him towards the true story of the vanished 'Princess'.

On the night when he had discovered Fleur's strange disappearance, he had been the most baffled and astounded man on the Côte d'Azur. It was hard for him to credit the story which his men told—that they had gathered on the moonlit terrace of the Hôtel de Paris according to his instructions, only to find that she was not there. Manton had cursed them roundly, suggesting in forcible language that they were a lot of incompetent fools.

It was not until he heard the count's version of the incident that he was persuaded that his own men were telling the truth. Fleur's French dancing-partner was rushing around the gardens in a state of great agitation, bewailing the fact that *la belle princesse* had been carried off by masked men.

There had been a large number of men, he asserted. He had been hopelessly outnumbered, and had deemed it more practical to raise a general alarm. By the time he returned to the gardens with help there was no sign of life, only the sound of a high-powered car being driven rapidly up the hill towards the Boulevard des Moulins.

'*Je n'ai pu rien faire,*' he cried.

Manton and the men who were to be handsomely paid to carry out the job, met and discussed the situation. They also were in a state of intense agitation. Nothing had been left to chance; of that they were certain. They had entered the hotel gardens at the exact moment. It was not their fault, they argued, if the bird had flown. They had taken

153

considerable risk and would make it highly uncomfortable for all concerned if their money was not forthcoming.

There was nothing for Manton to do but pay up and begin enquiries. At first he was puzzled, then furious, as it became increasingly obvious that he must realise his publicity stunt had been forestalled. The incident which he had meant to be a well-planned fake had become fact. Fleur had, apparently, been spirited away, she had genuinely vanished. How and where he could not think.

At first he half hoped that she was playing a joke; that she would turn up again later that night. But she did not come back, and as the count broadcast the story of his adventures in the garden to everybody he met in Monte Carlo, the news spread like wildfire and was public property by the following day. The incident was discussed at every dinner-table. Fleur had her publicity, Manton reflected grimly. Publicity of the wrong kind.

He and his friends from the Balham studios stood by in impotent dismay and wonder. By mutual consent they did not reveal the fact that Fleur was a film-actress. The papers published the news that a *distinguished foreign princess* had been abducted in the middle of a ball at the Hôtel de Paris. The authorities in Monaco were said to be making an energetic and exhaustive search for her, and had the matter well in hand.

The next day Manton had the unpleasant task of communicating with his chief in London, and with Fleur's family. The former confessed himself as puzzled and worried as his publicity-man. The tables had been properly turned on them. At the moment there was nothing for them to do but sit tight and wait for her to reappear, then, if possible, carry on with the film. Manton would have liked to have said that he had no intention of staying a moment longer on the Italian frontier, but a suggestion from the chief that there might conceivably be better publicity-men looking for a job forced him to climb down.

The film company decided that it would be fatal to let Fleur's mother know at this stage that her daughter was, in truth, lost. Such a revelation would lead to a much more extensive search being organised, a public enquiry and a scandal which would put an end to all their hopes of making the film a commercial success. If the truth became public, it would not only make them the laughing-stock of the profession, but would probably lead them into court with the possibility of having to pay out extensive damages. The chief hinted that Manton might even find himself in the dock at the Old Bailey answering a charge of abduction, which had been known to lead to prison.

Manton waited for Fleur in a state of painful anxiety. Every hour he expected her to turn up, and every hour added to his steadily mounting fears. His anxiety was not only born of the desire to carry out his contract and retain his job with the studios. It sprang from a deeper and fiercer feeling. The feeling that he must get her back for himself. Once he found her, the studios could go to the devil. There was always another job to be found, but there was only one Fleur.

In his heart he guessed that Blake Carew was implicated, if not the main cause of the whole business. It was obvious to the whole world that Blake had been in love with Fleur and one of the first things Manton did after his disappearance was to communicate with the millionaire's secretary. On being told that Mr. Carew had sailed on his yacht for an unknown destination, and that nobody knew when he would be back, Manton was frankly suspicious.

It was only natural that he should connect her absence with Blake's departure, but as he knew nothing definite, he could not act. He was forced to remain at the hotel, killing time, gloomily reading the newspaper reports and cursing his luck.

He did not believe that Fleur—was entirely to blame. She had always been meticulous in carrying out her part of the contract, carrying it out to the letter. She might have been tempted to do something foolish, he thought, but it was highly improbable that she would deliberately sacrifice her whole future career

156

because of a passing infatuation for the young Englishman. It was more likely that Blake had involved her in some hair-brained escapade which she would bitterly regret.

Manton finally came to the conclusion that he could not afford to stay at the most expensive hotel in Monte Carlo for much longer. The chief was already grumbling about the amount of expenses which had been incurred, and it was no use trying to conceal the fact that the publicity stunt had cost the studios a lot of money. Now it looked as though the whole thing had been a lamentable waste of time and cash.

By the end of the week, when there was still no news of Fleur, and the local police confessed themselves defeated and without a single clue to work on, Manton was forced to communicate once again with London. This time the truth could no longer be kept from Fleur's family, and an hour after her mother and sister learned that she had vanished, the affair was in the hands of Scotland Yard.

The story about the fake princess was published on both sides of the Channel, and the directors of the film studios were not only forced to admit that the whole thing was a tragedy from their point of view, but were prepared to accept the most unpleasant consequences.

The latest news of the war, and the apparent hopelessness of the search, made

Manton decide to leave for England without delay. It was not an inviting prospect which lay ahead of him. The trip would be long and dangerous, and his reception at the other end frigid—but anything was better than staying on in France under the present circumstances. Hanging about a town a bare five miles from a country which had declared war against yours was not Manton's idea of getting the most out of life. If it had not been for his work, he reflected ruefully, he would have been sitting safely and comfortably in his London flat. It seemed to him that Fleur and the Axis were contriving to make things as difficult as possible.

Monte Carlo was now a veritable city of the dead. Manton was the sole remaining guest in his hotel, which was obviously preparing to shut its doors. The Casino was closed down and stood silent and mournful at the far end of the deserted Camembert. There was only one bar remaining open where he could get a drink.

When he heard that the train services might be curtailed, he decided to move to Cannes. There were still a good number of British subjects there. He would be able to find someone to talk to and share his troubles, and he would be further removed from the frontier. The fact that he could look straight into Italy from his bedroom window in the hotel was a never-ending source of horror to him. It was so easy to imagine those heavy

158

guns on the Alpes-Maritimes which were probably pointing straight towards his room at this very moment.

He found a taxi-driver who would take him to Cannes for five hundred francs, and instructed the man to go to the Hôtel Suisse, where the men who had helped him with the kidnapping plot were staying. It would be more pleasant to stay there and he would leave word with the Monegasque police to let him know if they had any word of Fleur.

The drive along the twisting coastal road helped to convince him that he had been wise in leaving. On five different occasions the car was stopped at hastily erected barricades, while his papers and passport were examined. In Cannes the people in the streets looked around them with sheer despair. Not a smiling face was to be seen. It was Manton's first experience of a country which was writhing in its death-agonies, and the atmosphere of gloom added to his already heavy depression.

As they drove along the Croisette they came towards a crowd which surged round a small building and stretched across the road. Manton recognised many people whom he had seen in Monte Carlo, and tapping against the window called on the driver to stop.

'What's happened?' he asked in execrable French. 'They are all British people, by the look of them. What are they doing?'

The driver braked his car and shrugged his

shoulders.

'It is the British Consulate, *monsieur*. Perhaps the people have had orders to leave the country.'

Manton did not wait to hear more. Jumping from the car, he thrust five hundred francs into the man's hand and began to push his way through the chattering crowd. On the steps of the Consulate he found one of his own men sitting on a suit-case trying to shade his head with a newspaper from the glare of the morning sun.

'What the hell's going on here, Brent?' Manton asked urgently.

The man put down his paper with an exclamation of surprise.

'So you made it! We thought you were fixed in Monte for the duration. How did you get the news?'

'I didn't get any news,' Manton exploded. 'That's what I'm asking you for. What is this blasted circus?'

'The last of the money-giving English,' Brent smiled. 'Have you not noticed the depression in the town? The people think our suit-cases are filled with gold. We've been given notice to quit the country. Our last chance, old boy. The alternative is a Wop concentration camp.'

Manton put down his case and wiped his forehead with a handkerchief. His anger at the prospect of a last-minute flight with its obvious dangers and hardships was only tempered by the knowledge that he might have been left behind. But the voyage home sounded none too healthy. There were a few small boats in the harbour, but no trace of an escort. If they were supposed to get through the Mediterranean without a convoy they would be a sitting target for the first Italian submarine which spotted them.

'Thank heavens, I got here,' he muttered. 'I had no idea things were so far gone. The *Continental Daily Mail* was unobtainable, and I can't make sense of those French rags.'

The news which Brent imparted could hardly have been more disturbing. It meant the subjugation of France. The war in the West had been brought to an end after barely six weeks of fighting. The Bordeaux government had capitulated and were making a pitiful bargain for a pitiless peace. A bargain which placed the bulk of France's economic and war machine at the disposal of the Nazis, to be used against the common enemy.

Brent affirmed that the people had been sold by their politicians. Already General de Gaulle had broadcast an appeal from London, asking Frenchmen in the colonies and all parts of the world to rally in defence of their country. The fire of French resistance, he said, must flame and burn.

Manton had never heard of General de Gaulle, but the knowledge that the colonies were expected to go on fighting was a slight comfort. They were a comparatively short distance from North Africa. Once they got there they could stay safely and comfortably until the naval authorities at Gibraltar could arrange to send an escort for them. It was the prospect of the trip to Algeria which worried him. They might pick up a French destroyer at Marseilles, but nobody seemed sure of what the French navy meant to do, least of all Manton, who had had his confidence badly shaken as far as anything to do with France was concerned.

Not until he saw a British flag, or set foot on British soil, would he know any real peace of mind. And even then one couldn't know what lay in store. If they did manage to get back to England they would probably arrive just in time to meet the full weight of the blitzkrieg or invasion.

It was a gloomy outlook. An outlook which was not helped when they walked down to the harbour where they were to embark. The boat which had been sent to take them to an unknown destination turned out to be a four thousand ton collier which had recently brought a cargo of coal from Wales. It had a crew of twenty, lifeboat accommodation for thirty and no lifebelts.

It looked as though there must be over four hundred passengers scrambling for places on her steel decks. They were all British nationals, mostly residents from the Riviera, and many elderly or infirm women.

There was no sleeping accommodation. The passengers were given the choice of going down a perpendicular ladder to a dark, dust-filled hold or sleeping on deck in any vacant spot. Manton chose the latter. If they ran into trouble there would be little chance of being saved, but anything was better than being trapped like a rat in a cage.

The final scene as they lay at anchor in the harbour under the shade of the *Casino Municipal* was Dantesque in its pathos. The Navy—the first and last hope of every stranded Briton—was conspicuous by its absence. They were ready to sail, when a tug, its decks crowded with a motley collection of refugees of every nationality, nosed its way alongside. The collier's captain took a megaphone and pointed to the flag of the merchant navy which floated from the mast. Only British nationals were allowed to be taken on his ship. The people in the smaller boat wept with despair, and Manton knew that he would never forget the anguished look on the faces that stared up at him from the tug.

Manton was a confirmed social-climber who had a frank reverence for Debrett. Under any other conditions he would have found this voyage a readymade opportunity for making contact with people whose names and faces were known in every society magazine. A world-famous author sat talking with the manager of the British garage at Monte Carlo. An Indian prince, whose fortune was known to run into millions, shared a tin of condensed milk with the professional from the Mont Agel golf-course, and discussed the games which they would play together at St. Andrews after their return to England.

If they returned to England! The boat was a hotbed of wildly fantastic rumours. It was whispered that they were bound for Canada, and that the French fleet had been taken over by the Germans and would prevent their passage up the English and Irish Channels. One elderly Englishwoman who was supposed to be on speaking terms with the captain suggested that they were to be left at Corsica for the duration of the war.

At the end of the third day the food shortage became acute. Most of the passengers had taken some tins of food and bottles of water, but Manton had not had time to buy anything. Somehow the crew repeated the miracle of feeding the five thousand, with what at first appeared to be little more than home-made loaves and tinned fishes. It was a monotonous and tasteless diet, but it was sufficient to support the passengers who had settled down without a murmur to brave torpedoes, mines and bombs, and taking it in turns to keep submarine watch.

Manton felt that he could have put up with

the discomfort without the danger, or the danger without the discomfort. Both at once made a difficult pill to swallow. The discomfort was certainly acute. Coal dust penetrated to every part of the boat and begrimed them all. When they ran into heavy weather there was a lot of illness. The men from the Balham studios were not students of human nature, but they had to admit that the trip was a classic example of what people could endure.

The passengers were calm and unemotional. When warning of a hostile submarine was given, they watched the depth-charges being dropped with the same amount of interest as they would have displayed at the Derby or Ascot.

The British Vice-Consul from Nice was on board and spent his time walking around the decks, keeping up a flow of witty and encouraging conversation. On the morning of the fourth day he brought official news from the bridge. They were running into Oran, where everyone would be allowed to disembark and have a good meal. They might even stay there for some days. It all depended on the attitude which the French-colonies were taking up.

Less than an hour later the collier nosed its way behind a French cutter which piloted them through the harbour's mine-field. Manton saw the roofs of a straggling town reflected in the glaring sunlight, and turned to Brent, who sat struggling with a crossword puzzle in a ten days' old London newspaper.

'Get your things together,' he said with a sigh of relief. 'We'll be getting off in a few minutes. Think of it, my boy. Food and drink and a hot bath!'

Brent looked up from his paper and sucked the end of a pencil.

'A word of six letters?' he asked. 'Meaning "Ceases to exist".'

'France!' said Manton.

* * *

The French authorities at Oran were effusive in their welcome to the crowd of unwashed British refugees who swarmed over the landing-stage. Customs formalities were waived. There were large open boxes of cigarettes from which everyone was asked to help themselves. A fleet of cars waited to take the passengers to hotels and billets in the town. There was no talk of surrender amongst the local inhabitants, only optimism and a feeling of irrepressible gaiety.

Manton and Brent were driven to a hospital where baths, clean clothes and a meal of coffee, omelettes and bread awaited them. Everything worked with clockwork efficiency. This was not the first time that Oran had handled refugees. More than eight hundred had arrived during the week.

The streets and cafés of the town were crowded. After a bath and shave Manton and Brent walked along the main street. They had a certain amount of French money which they intended to spend, being convinced that by the time they reached England the franc would be valueless.

Entering a café where a band was playing Algerian music they sat down at the only remaining table and ordered a bottle of red wine. The waiter was pouring it out when Brent suddenly pointed across the smoke-filled room.

'Isn't that Bob Swan?' he exclaimed.

Manton peered across the haze and recognised one of the men whom the studios had selected to help him with the kidnapping plot.

'Sure, it is,' he answered, rising to his feet. 'Where the devil did he come from?'

Swan looked up with a start to find the publicity-man leaning over his table.

'Mr. Manton! This is a great break. I reckoned you were stuck in France. When'd you get here?'

'An hour ago. On the collier. How long have you been around?'

'Since Tuesday. They brought us over on a troop-ship. It's a hell of a one-horse town. What do you think about Miss Lorraine and Carew?'

Manton straightened up with a jerk, the

blood racing to his temples.

'Miss Lorraine! Carew!' he repeated. 'I know nothing about them. I've had no news. What are you talking about?'

Swan lit a foul-smelling Algerian cigarette. The fact that he had the advantage of Manton, whom he thoroughly disliked, pleased and flattered him. It had been obvious to them all that their publicity-man was not only in love with Fleur Lorraine but was in the studio black-books.

The story which the executive told was short and to the point. A boatload of exhausted Italian sailors had been found on the Cap Martin beach. After having been revived and interrogated by the *gendarmerie*, they explained that they were the crew of Blake Carew's yacht. They had mutinied and deserted when it became apparent that Italy was entering the war on the side of the Axis. Further enquiries by the police elicited the staggering information that an S O S had been received from the yacht stating that she was out of control and likely to founder at any moment. Her position was given as some twenty miles due east of Oran on the Algerian coast.

'So it was Blake Carew who pipped us on the post,' Swan concluded. 'I always thought he had an eye for the beautiful Fleur.'

'Don't worry about what you thought,' Manton snapped. 'Did the men say what attitude she took up?'

Swan nodded. He knew that Fleur had been overheard calling Blake every abusive name under the sun, but he had no intention of giving Manton the satisfaction of thinking that she had been upset. He chose his words carefully, watching the other man's every reaction.

'She appears to have cut up rough at first,' he said slowly. 'One of the Wops said she tried to escape, but after that she seems to have settled down quite happily. She's probably living comfortable at the moment.'

Manton looked him straight in the eyes.

'You mean they may still be alive?'

'Why not? Just because the yacht sunk it doesn't mean that they went down with it. There were lifeboats. They could probably swim. I certainly don't see why they should be written off the map.'

'In that case we'll try to get to them.'

Swan's eyes narrowed. Old Manton must really be in a bad way if he were suggesting setting out on a search. Well, let him get on with it—alone! Swan had had enough excitement of late—more than enough to last him for a long time. If the love-stricken fool wanted to risk his neck in a mad escapade, he would have to do it on his own. Oran was no picnic, but it was preferable to sailing down a mine-infested coast trying to find another fellow's girl.

'It would be a waste of time, Mr. Manton.

They may have worked their way inland. It would be like looking for a needle in a haystack.'

'That may be,' Manton returned. 'But it's worth trying. We'll make a bid for it as soon as possible.'

'Please yourself, sir. You can count me out.'

Manton's eyes blazed with anger.

'You'll do what I tell you.'

Swan shook his head.

'I take my orders from the studios, not from you. I wasn't brought out here to spend my time running after your girl friend.'

Manton tried to control his temper. He knew that the fellow was speaking the truth. There was no way he could force him to help. In Oran a film-magnate was just another refugee. It would be different in England when the young fool could be dealt with in no uncertain fashion.

Striding across the room, Manton returned to the table where Brent had finished most of the wine. He sat down and gulped the contents of his glass. His hands were shaking, his face tense with excitement.

Brent looked at him curiously.

'What's the matter? You look as though you'd seen a ghost.'

'I've heard about one. Fleur! She's supposed to be stranded about twenty miles from here.'

Brent whistled through his teeth. This was

news. He was silent while Manton told the story which he had heard from Swan. Not until it came to the part about searching for Fleur did he speak. It sounded a tricky proposition. If they set off down the coast it was quite possible that the last boat for England would sail from Oran, leaving them stranded. The situation did not appeal to Brent. He was all for getting hold of Fleur, and collecting gratitude and a fat reward from both Manton and the studios, but neither of these things would avail him if he found himself left in Algeria for the rest of the war.

The latest news had not been encouraging. The Bordeaux government had told all Frenchmen in the colonies that it was their duty to surrender. The local inhabitants admitted that they were beginning to waver. If they were true patriots, they argued, they should obey their government. But if they resisted or helped the Allies, the Germans would certainly look after their relations and property in France with typical Nazi brutality.

'It's not so easy as it sounds,' Brent said. 'We don't want to be stuck here, do we?'

Manton shook his head. He was eminently one to agree with Brent's safety-first sentiments, but he felt that there must be some way out. Already the germ of an idea was forming in his mind. It was an idea by which he would get back to England—with Fleur.

'Listen,' he said, leaning confidentially

across the table. 'If we can find the boat which is scheduled to take us home we've only got to see the captain and explain what's happened.'

'Explain what's happened!' Brent repeated incredulously. 'It'll make a pretty queer-sounding story.'

'We can tell an expurgated version of the story. You don't expect me to tell him we're interested in her publicity.'

Brent listened with interest to what the elder man had to say. He had never had a high opinion of Manton's capabilities, but he had to admit that the publicity-man was capable of producing an occasional flash of genius. The plan of campaign which Manton now unfolded sounded safe and promising.

Fleur was a British national, Manton reminded him. That would be his ace card. He would manage to get in touch with whatever British ship arrived for them, and tell the captain that Fleur was known to be a short sailing time down the coast. No man would refuse to help a woman in such circumstances. When he had persuaded the captain to make this slight deviation of course, he would make a quick search for Fleur. If he found her, all would be well. If not they would go back to the ship and return to England.

'It's certainly an idea,' admitted Brent. 'But hadn't you better say that you're a relation of hers?'

Manton smiled.

'Sure, I will. I'll say she's my wife. It may be a bit of wishful thinking, but it'll save a lot of complications.'

'There's just one thing you forgot.'

'What is it?'

'Carew!'

Manton signed to the waiter and ordered a second bottle of wine. Not until the man had filled their glasses and left their table did he reply.

'I don't owe Blake Carew anything,' he said evenly. 'I only intend to get Fleur and hold on to her. Carew has got himself into a tight corner. As far as I'm concerned, he can stay there. In fact, I think we can arrange for him to stay there for a very long time!'

CHAPTER TEN

On the opposite side of the woods in which Blake and Fleur were existing, two men were mooring a small boat which they had just rowed to shore. They had worked swiftly and noiselessly under a sky of stars and moonlight, but now as they landed the moon was suddenly hidden behind a bank of cloud, and darkness descended on the country.

About half a mile out from the shore lay a ship, the dimmed lights at her masthead twinkling and gleaming like rosy eyes in the velvet night. The man who appeared to be the leader of the expedition stared round him for a second or two as though allowing his eyes to get accustomed to the darkness, then beckoned to the other to follow him.

'This is undoubtedly the spot where we should come across them,' he said. 'Or we may find someone who can tell us exactly what has happened. I'm certain that was Carew's yacht which we saw foundering on the rocks. If anyone was saved from it they must be out here.'

Brent looked towards Mark Manton and nodded.

'This is the spot all right,' he agreed. 'We'd better begin to search. What about shouting Carew's name?'

'I don't care a damn about Carew,' Manton said, leading the way from the beach up to the luxuriant growth of trees and bushes beyond. 'I've already told you that. All I want to know is that Fleur is alive.'

It did not take long to get through the narrow strip of woodland which bordered the sea. The captain had given them permission to stay for an hour, but it was less than twenty minutes later that they came upon the figure of a girl lying fast asleep under a man's coat. Manton pulled an electric torch from his pocket, and running forward, flashed it on her face. One glance at the beautiful curve of cheek and mouth, the curling lashes and chestnut curls, was enough. He turned to Brent, a low cry of triumph on his lips.

'What did I tell you! It's her. It's Fleur . . .'

Once again he repeated her name, and this time the girl sat up with a violent start, her heart racing with fear and shock.

'Blake . . .' she began, then paused as she became aware that she was staring up into the familiar face of Mark Manton. 'My God—it's *you!*'

'Yes, it's Mark,' he said, laughing with relief and excitement. 'Thank heaven I've found you. Are you all right? Tell me about yourself— what you've been doing—how you got here?'

For a moment Fleur was incapable of speech. She struggled to her feet and continued to stand staring at him. It seemed incredible that this man in the dirty torn clothes was Mark Manton, and that he had discovered her in this desolate part of the world.

'I can't believe it,' she said, as though speaking to herself. 'It's amazing! How did *you* get *here*? How?'

'By a miracle,' Manton said. 'Look here, Fleur, this is not the time to discuss details. I don't know what explanations you've got to give for what you did at Monte Carlo, and I don't much want to hear it now, but I'll tell you my story if you want to know it.'

'Go on. Tell me.'

Manton leaned against the trunk of a tree and lit a cigarette. They had plenty of time

175

before they need return to the boat. He felt he could do with a rest after the excitement of the last few minutes, and it would be advisable to give Fleur some indication of the attitude which she should take up with the captain.

The story which he told her began with the flight from France and their arrival at Oran. Fleur heard about the Italian crew being found, and the yacht's S O S, and how Manton had moved heaven and earth to find the captain of the ship which was now to take them back to England. At first he said it had seemed as though they would be forced to abandon the search, but the publicity-man's glib tongue and powers of persuasion had won the day. The captain had agreed to anchor off this part of the coast for one hour, during which Manton and Brent would be allowed to take a small boat at their own risk and see what they could find.

'It was good of you, Mark,' Fleur broke in. 'I had begun to think I was here for keeps.'

He stepped forward, seizing both her bare arms and holding her fast.

'I had only one desire in life, my dear—to find you again.'

'But how did you know the exact spot?'

'I saw the wreck of the yacht. For a moment I imagined you might be dead, but I presumed that if any of you had survived you would be about here. Thank heavens I was right.'

He tried to turn her face towards his and

kiss her. His eyes were glowing with excitement and passion. But she twisted out of his arms and pushed him away.

'Don't, please . . .'

'Come, Fleur.' He moved his head impatiently. 'Don't ride the high horse. I've risked my life to rescue you. You must realise that. And you know why I did it. Because I love you. I loved you in Monte Carlo. You treated me badly there. You put me on one side, but you can't do so now. I've found you and I'm going to keep you.'

'You're wrong if you think that. You seem to forget that I'm not alone here.'

'You mean Carew is here?'

'Of course I do.'

'Where is he?'

She looked over her shoulder.

'Somewhere about. I don't know exactly where. I haven't seen him since we said good night.'

A glitter of rage showed in Manton's eyes.

'Carew carried you off—by force,' he said. 'The crew who mutinied said you were scared to death, that you loathed him and tried to escape. Isn't that true?'

'It may have been, but . . .'

'But you didn't find him quite the charming hero you thought him in Monte Carlo! The man who wanted Princess Fleur wasn't so keen about Miss Lorraine of Streatham!'

Fleur's cheeks flushed scarlet. She had a

sudden burning desire to defend Blake now and always. There was no real reason why she should hide her feelings from Mark or any other man.

She said haughtily:

'I really don't see that it's any concern of yours. But if you want to know, Blake and I understand each other.'

'Drop the drama,' Manton cut in. 'And don't try and pull the sob-sister act. It doesn't suit you, darling. You're coming straight back to the ship with me, and back to England. When we get there you are going to marry me.'

She looked at him with indignation in her eyes.

'You're behaving like a lunatic.'

Manton laughed.

'The little drama isn't over yet, my dear. We'll make it a finer one than anything the studios have yet turned out. You will continue to play the lead. But I direct it this time, you understand? Not Carew.'

Fleur shrank back and looked nervously from him to Brent, who appeared to be waiting at a distance for orders. Was it possible that they meant to take her to the ship by force? Surely she had had enough of being taken places against her will. She did not intend to let it happen again.

Suddenly she raised her voice.

'Blake!' she called. 'Blake!'

Manton swung round towards Brent.

'Take her arms,' he said curtly.

The next moment Fleur found herself struggling with the men. It was a struggle which was short-lived. Brent was a strong man and fight as she would she was powerless in his grip. A hideous feeling of fear engulfed her.

'I'll go with you,' she said, turning her eyes to Manton. 'I'll go when you've found Blake.'

'Your beloved Blake can look after himself.'

'Please, Mark,' she said breathlessly. 'You must take him. You can't leave him here alone. He might never get away. You must realise that.'

'I realise that he began this abduction business and now he can make the best of it and stay here until . . .'

Manton never finished his sentence. Somewhere close at hand they heard a shout. There was the sound of a clump of bushes being torn apart. Fleur and the two men swung round to see Blake coming towards them.

Blake looked slightly confused. He was dishevelled and heavy-eyed, as though he had woken suddenly from a deep sleep. Rubbing his eyes, he stared amazedly from Fleur towards the men. Then he saw and recognised Manton.

'I'll be damned,' he drawled. 'If it isn't our old publicity-hound himself! Who do we have to thank for this surprise?'

'You don't have to thank anyone,' Manton returned grimly. 'I came here to get Fleur.

She's returning to England with me.'

Blake turned to Fleur.

'What's he talking about? How did he get here?'

'He found out from your crew who got us here,' she said frantically. 'He has followed us to get me away. Don't let him take me, Blake. Don't let him.'

Blake's grey eyes shone. The very foundation of his heart was shaken by her words and the expression on her face. So she didn't hate him so very much. She did not want to leave him, in fact—or to let Manton rescue her.

'My dear, if you don't want to go with Manton, you need not,' he said calmly.

'And how will you stop her?' asked Manton, sneering.

'*Like this!*'

Fleur saw Blake make a spring towards Manton. Then the men were down together on the grass, their arms and legs interlocked, until Blake's strong fingers found his opponent's throat. Fleur felt a wave of pride and exultation. Blake was the man she loved and he was fighting—fighting for her.

In her excitement she forgot that Brent was standing beside her. When she remembered him it was too late. The fight which Blake was obviously winning with comparative ease was brought to a sudden horrible finish. It was Brent who lifted a stone and flung it at the young Englishman's head. Blake gave a groan, and falling backwards, crumpled up on the ground.

Manton rose painfully to his feet, his breath coming in short gasps.

'Thanks, Brent,' he said, when he was sufficiently recovered to speak. 'I think that has put paid to our wealthy friend. Give me a hand with the girl.'

Fleur felt herself being lifted and held in strong arms. She uttered scream after scream, her eyes riveted on Blake's prone body. She knew now how desperately she loved him. To leave him there hurt and perhaps dying, while she was taken forcibly away by Manton, filled her with an agony of despair.

'Blake,' she sobbed. *'Blake!'*

But even as she called that name she realised that he lay where he could not hear her voice, and that later tonight, when the moon rode triumphantly over the clouds and shone down on the forest, there would be only one human being here. An insensible man with blood pouring from an old wound in his head, reopened by the blow he had just received.

And that was the one man whom she loved and who was also the one in her life whom she ever would love.

*   *   *

Locked in Mark Manton's cabin, still in her

torn black dress and without shoes or stockings, Fleur paced up and down, wondering feverishly how she could escape.

She could feel the vibration of the engines, and guessed that the ship was putting out to sea. That meant that she was going further away from the coast—and from Blake.

The longer she visualised him lying where they had left him, injured and perhaps unconscious, the more intense grew her desire to return at all costs and save him. She loved him. Now that Manton had dragged her forcibly away from him she knew just how utterly and completely she cared. She no longer bothered about safety or liberty. Pride ceased to matter. She only wanted to get away from this hateful ship and get back to Blake, stay with him on that desolate stretch of land, if need be, for the rest of her life. It would not matter to her if she had to remain a virtual prisoner for the duration of the war, so long as Blake was with her. The strip of Algerian coast which had once seemed a grim, impossible spot, cutting her off from civilisation and humanity, had become her paradise. It drove her insane now to feel herself being taken steadily away from it.

Somebody turned the handle of her door and opened it gently. Fleur stood still, her hands clasped convulsively behind her back. Her face was white and disfigured with tears, but when she saw that it was Manton who was entering the cabin, she dug her nails into her palms and faced him calmly. She was not going to show fear to this man who dared to keep her locked in his cabin, and who imagined he was going to retain possession of her.

'Well, my dear,' Mark said amiably, and shut the door behind him and turned the key, 'feeling more resigned?'

She said:

'I advise you to stop this play-acting.'

'Oh, come.' Manton approached her with a swagger, and removing the stump of a cigar from his mouth, laid it on an ash-tray and held out his hands to her. 'My dearest child, you can't pretend you want to return to that playboy who fooled around with you in Monte Carlo. I have rescued you, Fleur—saved you.'

'Then you can un-rescue me,' she said childishly and near to tears. 'I don't thank you for your brave conduct. You're a low coward. You left a man on that coast, hurt and possibly dying.'

'I should worry!'

She looked at his mean, malicious face in disgust.

'How I loathe you!'

'Don't be silly,' said Manton. 'I'm a rich man and I can give you all that you want. I may not be a millionaire like Carew but . . .'

'You poor fool!' she interrupted fiercely. 'Do you really imagine in your perverted brain that I'd touch your money?'

'You always wanted expensive things and a good time. When you were at the studios you sighed for money and what it can bring. You took on the job as the fake princess and obviously revelled in the luxury which it gave you.'

'That was my job.'

'Don't be futile. You can't manage to impress me with the idea that you're really in love with Carew. The crew of his yacht said that you created the devil's own row when you were locked in *his* cabin. You hated him.'

She flushed hotly and now tears sprang to her eyes.

'I was never locked in his cabin. When he took me away I naturally resented it. He misunderstood my attitude, and you helped to widen the breach by telling him that I was going to marry you. Now we both know the truth, and we love each other.'

'You are going to marry *me*,' Manton said, trying to take her in his arms. 'When you have had time to calm down and see things in their proper perspective you will realise that I have always been your friend. You said so in London.'

'In London you were a rational being—not the raving lunatic which you are now,' she said, struggling in his arms. 'Let me go. If you don't I'll have the whole crew down here. This ship can't be full of swine like yourself. There'll be someone who won't stand for it.'

Manton muttered an oath and released her. Had she but realised it, Fleur was dealing with the situation in the best possible way from her point of view. By taking up a strong, defensive attitude, she had Manton beaten. He had counted on the act that her relief at being saved would render her meekly acquiescent. She had guessed correctly. There were plenty of men and women on the ship who would whisper among themselves and raise their brows if they heard a girl screaming.

Manton tried to hide his alarm. He had told the captain that Fleur was his wife and that she was in a somewhat hysterical state, but he did not want a scene to take place. He determined to try less drastic measures.

'Listen to me, Fleur,' he said in an ingratiating voice. 'Be sensible, and forget about this man. When we get to London I will marry you.'

'You never will. I advise you to get me off this ship,' she retorted, eyeing him steadily. 'If you don't, I shall give you in charge for assaulting Blake. If he is found dead, you will hang for it.'

Manton blanched.

'You're hysterical!'

'I meant it,' Fleur warned him. 'Now you know what I intend to do.'

'If you take up that line, I'll merely say that I hit him in self-defence. Brent will uphold me. I can prove I saved you. Everyone knows that the "fake princess" was kidnapped. They can soon be informed that Carew was responsible. I shall be acclaimed as a hero.'

Her eyes flashed contemptuously.

'What a hero!' she jeered.

Manton's face grew livid with rage. He flung his arms around her and pressed his lips against her flushed cheek.

'Damn you, you shan't get the better of me. I've gone through hell to find you and save you. Now I . . .'

Fleur gave one scream.

'Help!'

A moment later footsteps came running along the corridor outside the cabin. Manton, shaking and impotent with rage, let her go. He hurriedly unlocked the door and looked out. A white-coated steward was coming towards them.

'It's all right, steward,' said Manton. 'My wife has not been well. Shock, you know. But she's all right now. I'm taking care of her.'

The steward nodded and went away. It seemed a pretty queer-looking affair to him, but he had been well trained to mind his own business and intended to do so.

Manton waited until the man had left before attempting to relock the cabin door. But this time he was too late. With a sudden rush Fleur was past him before he could grip her arms or stop her. She ran frenziedly down the corridor towards the deck, screaming as she ran.

The captain, talking to one of his officers at the foot of the bridge, heard the shrill cries and hastened to see what was wrong. He met a strange apparition at the end of the deck. Fleur in her torn clothes, a slim black figure in the blaze of moonlight, curly chestnut hair in wild disorder, eyes dimmed with tears. She stumbled towards him with a sob.

'Help me, please, whoever you are. Take me back to shore.'

Captain Hobson, an elderly, grey-bearded seaman, quickly took the trembling little hand which was thrust out to him.

'My dear young lady,' he began kindly, 'what on earth is the matter?'

Before Fleur could reply, Manton arrived flushed and out of breath.

'Go back to your cabin, Fleur,' he commanded.

Fleur clung to the captain's arm.

'No, no! Don't let him take me. You must help me—take me back to the land.'

Captain Hobson looked at them both with concern.

'What is the trouble?' he asked, addressing himself to Manton.

'It's all right, Captain. My wife has had a difficult time.' Manton touched his forehead significantly. 'Shock, you know, after all she's gone through.'

'Poor girl,' said the captain. 'I see what you mean.'

'I'm not mad. It isn't true,' Fleur cried. 'I'm as sane as you are and I am not his wife. For God's sake believe and listen to me. A man has been left on that coast, left there seriously wounded. He's an Englishman. This man who calls himself my husband attacked him. We must go back. We can't leave him there to die.'

Captain Hobson's face expressed astonishment and concern.

'What have you to say about that, Mr. Manton?'

'There's not a word of truth in it. Can't you see that my wife is deranged, that she's not responsible for what she's saying? The man she speaks about was obviously drowned when the yacht sank. The tragedy of it all has been too much for her.'

The captain believed the story. He saw no reason to distrust Manton, whose wife was obviously in a precarious state of mind. Gently he disengaged himself from Fleur's clinging hands.

'My dear young lady, you must do what your husband advises. Go back to your cabin and have a good rest.'

'I tell you he isn't my husband,' she said in a desperate voice. 'If we had our passports I could prove it. I'm speaking the truth and I'm as sane as you are. Blake Carew has been left to die. He was alive when we left. I implore you to go back for him tonight or tomorrow.'

'My poor child,' said Manton in a soothing

voice, 'you hear what the captain has to say. You must come and lie down.'

She flung up her arms with a gesture of hopelessness.

'My God, how vile you are! Will nobody believe in me or help me?'

Manton literally dragged her back to the cabin. Not until she was inside and he had locked the door did he speak. Then he said triumphantly:

'You understand the position now! It's a waste of time to make a fuss. You'd do far better to accept things as they stand.'

'You vile beast!' she panted, striking at him with her clenched fist. 'You vile swine!'

He laughed.

'My dear, you'll settle down to it and feel much better and like your normal self in the morning. I won't offend you with any protests of affection tonight. I'm sure you must be tired. Go to sleep and wake up in a nicer mood. Good night.'

When he had left the cabin, Fleur flung herself on the bed in a seemingly endless passion of tears.

'Blake,' she sobbed, 'if you die, if you are already dead, then I want to die too.'

She was conscious of nothing save an overwhelming desire to be with him, to pillow that handsome head on her breast, to tell him at least once before she died that she loved him—to feel his kiss of pardon and

189

reconciliation on her lips, and give him hers.

CHAPTER ELEVEN

The long night passed. Fleur was awake with the first glimmer of dawn, once again pacing her cabin distractedly, haunted by the vision of Blake alone and injured in the woods. From her porthole she could just make out the distant fringe of palms on the shore. They had anchored all night. They were only a few miles from the land. It drove her desperate to think how near they were, yet how far removed she was from her lover.

Shortly before six o'clock she heard voices just outside her porthole. Eagerly she peered out and saw two sailors who were swabbing down the deck. The men were intent on their work and did not notice her looking at them, until she called in a low voice:

'Come here for a moment.'

The sailors looked up at the girl's pale, haggard face framed in the porthole.

'Good morning, miss,' one of them said.

'Listen,' said Fleur swiftly. 'Do you want to make some money—a lot of money?'

They exchanged glances, then came nearer.

'What do you mean?'

'I mean that there's a man on that bit of land—an Englishman who's been injured and left to die. I've got to save him.'

'That's a job for the captain, miss.'

'I know, I know,' Fleur replied impatiently. 'The Captain doesn't believe me. It's too long a story to explain now. I'm telling you the truth, I swear it. The man over there is Blake Carew, the millionaire.'

The spokesman of the two sailors looked interested.

'You don't mean Lieutenant-Commander Carew who was with the second destroyer flotilla at Scapa?'

Fleur nodded.

'He was in the Navy. Yes, I know he was at Scapa.'

'That puts a different complexion on things, miss. My son served with Lieutenant-Commander Carew. There's nothing I wouldn't do for him. He was good to my youngster.'

'Then will you take me?'

'It's a risk. If we were found out it would mean the sack.'

'Mr. Carew will look after you. I promise you that. If you get him away he'll give you enough money to buy a ship of your own.'

The sailor laughed and turned to his mate.

'What d'you say, George?'

'I'll take a chance.'

'Then we'd better look sharp. This is the best time to try. We should be back in half an hour.'

Fleur was in an agony of impatience. She

was trembling and flushed with hope. Perhaps she would save Blake yet. She prayed to God that they would find him safely.

Once the sailors had made up their minds to undertake the job, they acted promptly. Quietly and efficiently they let down one of the small boats, and within ten minutes had led Fleur from her cabin and lowered her over the side. While she had been waiting, Fleur had found a pen and notepaper and had written a note to the captain which she pushed under his cabin door. It was a note that she guaranteed would make him change his opinion about her state of mind, and keep the ship waiting for them.

The two sailors rowed well and energetically. The tide was in their favour and they were well on their way to the shore before signs of commotion on the ship showed that they had been discovered.

'That's torn it,' the one exclaimed. 'They've spotted us.'

The man was right. It was Mark Manton who, finding that Fleur was missing, rushed along the deck shouting at the top of his voice, towards the rowing-boat. Captain Hobson, half dressed and with a serious look on his weather-beaten face, came out of his cabin at the first sign of trouble. He held a note in his hand.

'Mr. Manton,' he said sternly, 'there are three hundred passengers on this ship trying to sleep. Will you please control yourself?'

'It's Fleur, my wife—she's gone!'

The captain nodded.

'I know that. She has told me about it.'

'What do you mean? Manton stammered.

'Read this.'

As Manton read what Fleur had written he knew that he was beaten.

I have persuaded two of your crew to take me to the shore. We will stay with Blake Carew unless he can be moved. You have only to send a boat to us to find out that I am speaking the truth.

Fleur Lorraine.

Manton crumpled up the note and shrugged his shoulders. His face was livid.

'You believe the ravings of a lunatic?' he said.

'I think I do,' said the captain coldly. 'Her note seems quite intelligent. My men must have been convinced or they would not have taken her there. However, we shall soon know. I must send a boat to her. Will you remain in your cabin until they return?'

Manton knew that this was the end. He had lost Fleur. There was only one vindictive hope left to him. That Blake Carew was dead, or died before she got to him.

As he sat disconsolately in his cabin, the sailors pulled the boat up on to the fine golden sands of the shore. Fleur's heart was hammering with excitement and fear. The fear that she might find Blake beyond help. She ran over the sunlit beach through the thickly spread palms towards the spot where she knew she would find him. Never had she run so quickly. Now she felt strong and capable of dealing with any emergency. She was ready for anything, any hardship, for his sake. The sailors followed her, glancing back towards the ship.

She found him lying on the ground as they had left him. In the bright morning sunlight he looked white and still, his hair matted with blood. She bent down on her knees beside him, calling his name.

'Blake, I'm here. Speak to me.'

There was no answer. No movement. No sign of life in his rigid body.

She turned to one of the sailors.

'What should we do?'

'I've got some rum, miss. Better try it.'

'Yes, quickly.'

The man took a bottle from his pocket and uncorked it. Fleur pillowed Blake's head on her shoulder and put it to his lips. The stillness of him suffocated her with fear. If he were dead it would be more than she could endure.

She poured a few drops of the brandy down his throat, and waited with her eyes on his face. Suddenly he coughed and stirred. Then his eyes opened and he was looking up at her dazedly. He felt her arms tighten about him, her warm tears on his cheek.

'Fleur . . .'

'Blake, my darling. Speak to me.'

He stretched a hand towards her.

'You're crying, Fleur. Don't cry. I love you.'

The sailor bent down and touched her shoulder.

'I shouldn't stay here, miss. The sooner you get him back to the ship the better. It's the Commander all right. Gawd! How did 'e get 'ere?'

Fleur ignored the question and told the sailors to pick up the injured man.

It was only a matter of minutes before they were all on board and she was sitting beside Blake's bed. Captain Hobson examined the wound and told her that there was nothing to worry about. Now that he was being looked after, Blake would soon be a different man, the captain assured her.

For the rest of that day Blake lay against his pillows, his hands locked in Fleur's. All his heart was in his eyes when he looked at her.

'My brave darling,' he whispered. 'So very brave.'

'Brave!' She laughed. 'You would have known there's nothing brave about me if you'd seen me last night.'

'What about Manton?'

'Forget about him,' she answered quickly. 'He's the captain's trouble now. He won't worry us again.

'It's a funny thing. The old devil and I have

both got one thing in common. We both tried to run away with you.'

'You didn't leave a man to die by himself. He's a swine—and you are . . .'

'What, darling?' Blake's grey eyes looked at her with mocking tenderness. 'You called me some unpleasant names a short while ago.'

'Don't, Blake.' She hid her face on his shoulder and both arms went round his neck. 'Darling, don't remember those things, *please.*'

'You love me now, Fleur?'

'You know I do.'

'My sweet!' He held her closer, shutting his eyes and kissing her hair. 'And I adore you.'

'Still, Blake?'

'More than ever. Let me hear you say you will marry me.'

'I shall have to, darling—because I can't live without you.'

'In that case, we will punish friend Manton by inviting him to our wedding and letting him see all the beauty, all the sweetness and enchantment which he has lost and I have won.'

She looked up at him with speechless worship in her eyes. Their lips met in a long deep kiss.

'Now I know happiness,' she whispered.

There was a gay, limitless light in his own eyes as they looked into hers.

'There's only one snag, my darling. I *can't* offer you a title—and you rather wanted to be a princess, didn't you?'